Applause for *The Village*

"*The Village* comes firmly out of a longstanding literary tradition. Hemingway's Nick Adams stories . . . and "The Bear" by Faulkner. . . . Mr. Mamet is well on his way to adding the fiction venue to his mastery of writing for the stage and screen."
   — Michiko Kakutani, *New York Times*

"Marvelous to behold. . . . Mamet's novel explores a community with its own laws, language, codes, habits, and sense of honor. It does so with the deft reverence for the real — Mamet's eye for detail and his ear for rhythms of vernacular speech are incomparable — coupled with a certain difficulty of approach, an avant-garde edge. What makes this seemingly paradoxical mix of techniques work is Mamet's appreciation of what it means to be human, how we survive, amid the detritus of the late 20th century. . . . It's a measure of Mamet's mastery of his new form, how wise and wonderful a novel he has written, that you can cut into *The Village* anywhere and find . . . moments of high art and basic humanity."
   — Douglas Glover, *Washington Post Book World*

"An impressive first novel."
   — *The Economist*

"Lean and taut and rife with imagery."
   — *Atlanta Journal and Constitution*

"The first novel from celebrated playwright David Mamet, about life in a remote New England town. As powerful and minimalist as his dramatic writing, it demonstrates that the author can write narrative as rich as his dialogue."
— *Stages, The National Theater Magazine*

"Strong and unsettling . . . lyrical marvels of description . . . Mamet has certainly got it right."
— *Louisville Courier Journal*

"David Mamet uses the people and voices in *The Village* as if he were hanging stars in the sky; not to illuminate themselves but to reveal the world by their faint light. . . . Mamet's writing is infused with a poetry that manages to be simultaneously hard-boiled and delicate."
— *Los Angeles Times*

"Not since Jack London has a writer captured snowscapes with such bone-chilling accuracy."
— *Baton Rouge Advocate*

"Amazing . . . masterful. . . . He unmasks a conversation the way those plate-glass exhibits in the zoo unmask a prairie dog's burrow."
— Bill McKibben, *New York Daily News*

"Worth settling in with on a long snowy night."
— *Boston Herald*

The Village

Also by David Mamet

The Village

A Novel

David Mamet

Little, Brown and Company

Boston New York Toronto London

First Paperback Edition

Library of Congress Cataloging-in-Publication Data

Mamet, David.
    The village : a novel / David Mamet. — 1st ed.
      p.   cm.
    ISBN 0-316-54572-4(HC)   0-316-54388-1(PB)
    1. Community life—New England—Fiction. 2. Villages—New England—Fiction. I. Title.
PS3563.A4345V5 1994
813'.54—dc20   94-4342

10 9 8 7 6 5 4 3 2 1

RRD-VA

Published simultaneously in Canada by Little, Brown & Company (Canada) Limited

Printed in the United States of America

This book is dedicated to Chris Kaldor

A swarm of bees in May is worth a load of hay.
A swarm of bees in June is worth a silver spoon.
A swarm of bees in July ain't worth a fly.

— folk saying

The Village

One

It became an increasingly clear parallelogram as he
watched it during the afternoon. And then it was gone.

He waited for it to return. He thought its disappearance had been caused by the wind moving the
shade, but then he realized it was a cloud which cut the
light off. His wife walked into the room.

"What are you doing?"

"Nothing," he said.

"How are you?"

"I'm fine. Much better."

She stood in the doorway. Not moving. As if there
were something to say, but she was not about to be the
one to say it. He felt guilty for a moment, as if his silence
were divisive.

"I'm ill," he said.

"I know that," she said; and then she was gone.

The parallelogram returned. Bright yellow where
he'd remembered it white. "No, it wasn't white," he
thought, "that wasn't how I remembered it. But more

white than it is." And he thought of the sky at sunset, when it goes white. "Yes," he thought. "It may be I'm the only one who knows that."

Deep in the covers there was sweat on his neck, and his bones ached.

"It hurts in my joints," he thought, "and I will never get to sleep. Why can I not get to sleep; why can I not get to sleep? I knew she would go. All that you have to do is wait, and it is always over.

"That's why I can't fall asleep, is that she may be back. Why would she do this?"

The pillow was hot, and he turned it; and the other side was hot.

"And now I'll never sleep because the bed is hot," he thought.

"There are things one can take. If there were someone to bring me an aspirin or a glass of cooling water." His mind fixed upon the thought of water, cool and cleansing him, and purifying him.

"A rest home," he thought. "Where there was no one to intrude," he thought. "Where their schedule was fitted to my rhythms. And they moved silently."

"Why would they do that?" he thought. "Are there people who so desire to serve?"

It was in Switzerland; and, in his mind, a deer looked up as he thought about it; though he wondered if there were sufficient habitat to support a deer herd that near the rest home.

"No. It would not do if they were there," he thought.

"If they were there, if they would come up to you. If

they were not frightened of you, or if there were two sorts of them, would they interbreed? If they did, what would be passed on? If they would come up to you?"

In his dream the deer and the sanitarium, and clean, heavy sheets became mixed with a cloud that was flat and white, and acted as a barrier, he thought, as he came awake to the shade snapping in the wind.

"Yes. As a barrier. Of course it would. As it is so thin."

He smiled at the simplicity of it.

"Yes," he thought. "The beauty of it. And I'd never noticed it before. Of course." And then he was asleep again.

The parallelogram of light moved to the angle of the wall, then up the wall, as he slept. Then the room was dark.

And when he woke there was a smell in the room which was not the clean sheets, nor the wind which blew up from the lake in his dream, but it was the smell of soup, and he did not like it.

He looked up at her.

"I cannot eat," he said.

"Well," she said.

He wanted to turn away and sleep, but he knew she would talk to him until she was satisfied. He searched for something to excuse himself.

"Do you want me to call a doctor?" she said.

"No."

"If that's what you want, tell me."

"No," he said; and thought he would give anything he owned if she would go away.

"No," he said, "I'm fine."

When he woke again the pillow was wet. His hair stuck to his head.

"How lovely," he thought, as his body relaxed. "Wouldn't that solve it."

But where would he put it, so that it would be there when he looked for it again; or, rather, so that he'd know where to look; for though it seemed so simple now, when much the focus of his existence was the bolt, what would he feel when he came back for it?

"I am sick of this life," he thought. "The more I know of myself the more I despise myself — for I see what I am, and, yet, am powerless to act to make it better."

"Now, we are swine," he thought, "and that's the root of it all. And that's why we like hunting. We're in competition with our betters."

On the street the girl walked by with a proclaimed unconsciousness of the havoc she was creating; as he got out of the truck and walked into the hardware store.

"You see that?" Dickie was saying as he walked in.

"What's that, Dick?" he said.

"Maris. *What's* her name . . . How you, then, Henry?"

"Yes. I saw her," he said. "Fine."

"Sweet, tight little thing."

"Yup."

"Don't half know everybody's looking at her."

"No, I'm sure she knows," Henry said.

"Lord, I would give the ten fifteen years it would cost just to go an hour with her."

"Would you, Dick?"

"Yes. I would."

". . . your *wife* say . . . ?"

"Wouldn't tell 'er." The two looked around as the door opened. A woman came into the store.

"Mornin', Chrissy," Dickie said, and turned back to Henry. ". . . help you with?"

"Need a nut for this bolt here," Henry said, and held up the bolt.

"What's it for?"

"You got one?"

"Sure."

Dickie walked Henry back to a wall of bins, and tried one, and then another nut from the various bins.

"What's it for?"

"Off a *trap* machine. Throws the clay pigeons."

"Do you need a washer?" Dickie asked.

"Well, sure."

Dickie searched in the bins and found the right nut, then dug a washer out of another bin, and handed them to Henry.

"You need help, Chrissy?" he called.

"I'm all right, Dick," she called back.

The two men walked back to the counter at the front of the store.

"Yup," Dick said.

". . . owe you?"

"Oh, nothin', I don't know. Twenty-nine cents. Pay me some other time, somethin' else. Look, there she goes."

The two men turned and watched the young girl walk by the plate glass window of the hardware store. They spoke out of the side of their mouths, as if they could hide the tone or subject of their conversation from the woman at the back of the store.

"Tell me now, Henry: what would you give. What would *you just give,* for one night with that little tart?"

The girl strode down the street. The customer called Dickie back to the back of the store, and he said, ". . . coming," and looked at the other man with a slight nod, as if to say "yessir."

Henry walked out on the street, to his truck parked by the gas pumps. He saw the girl's back as she walked along. He watched a moment, nodding, as if at the simple wisdom of some wise man's thought.

Dickie perched on the high stool by the cash register and watched the street.

On a pad in front of him were various figures written in pencil. Dickie looked down at the pad for a while. He circled a number on the pad, and then drew a line through it. The number represented the monthly mortgage payment on the store.

He reached behind him to a shelf where a pipe sat on a Bakelite pipe rest.

The pipe rest was a figure of a cartoon cowboy done in the oranges and greens of the 1930s. The cowboy had a broad smile, a blue bandanna, and a khaki hat. The pipe bowl lay in a depression at the cowboy's feet, and the stem rested on his shoulder. Dickie's hand came back and took the pipe. He filled it from a tin at his right hand. Next to the tin sat the pad with the mortgage figure. He filled and tamped his pipe while looking at the pad.

He stopped for a moment, and scratched his face, his eyes always on the pad. He started feeling on the counter for a match.

Outside, on the street, the girl, Maris, walked once more back from her mother's house to the post office. She passed the hardware store prepared to pay no mind to the man or men she knew would be watching for her. Her gaze, as usual, was straight ahead, right down the cracked sidewalk, past the hardware store, and the food store, to the post office, as if she were a model of imperturbable purpose.

But, as she sensed she was not being watched, her face would have shown, to the closest observer, the most minute sign of confusion in the slight tilt of her head — as if she were almost inclined to actually look to confirm her sense that she was not being watched.

Down at the post office Mrs. Bell stood across the counter from the Postmistress.

"Well, and if she don't want to see, well, then . . ."

"That's right," Mrs. Bell said.

"*I* don't know," the woman said, and she sighed.

"You could of told her back when she *met* him," Mrs. Bell said.

"Well, that's my point," the Postmistress said. "It's not what you *hear*. It is what you're prepared to *know*; and I'll tell you something else, though I don't like to say it, and it's always easier to say of someone else's problems than our own; but I don't know if, to a certain point, we don't choose our afflictions. Morning, Maris," the Postmistress said.

"Morning, Rose," the girl said.

"How is your mother?"

"Just fine. Mrs. *Bell* . . . ?"

"Good morning, Maris," Mrs. Bell said.

"What have you got, a *letter?*" the Postmistress said. "Give it to me." She took the letter and pulled out the stamp drawer. "That'll be twenty-nine cents," she said, and hefted the letter in her hand. "Better check it to make sure," she said. She laid the letter on the scale and nodded and said, "Twenty-nine cents."

The girl fished in the pocket of her jeans and brought out a small handful of change. She counted the money out and she laid it on the counter. "Thank you, Maris," the Postmistress said.

"Rose. Miz Bell . . ." the girl said, and walked out on the street, and flipped up the collar of her short red jacket.

The women waited until she was some steps away and then turned their heads ever so slightly, each toward the other, and each tightened her mouth and gave her head a small shake.

"And it's not right to expose the *girl* to it, too," the Postmistress said.

Back at the store Dickie was immersed in a catalogue. He made notes on a scratch pad assembled out of cut-up advertising flyers for store specials long past. He shook his head as he made his calculations, and did not raise his head as Maris walked past.

"Who is he kidding?" she thought; "And who does he think he is, and wouldn't I just like to get alone with him, in some *barn*, or some thing, and put him through an afternoon. What would he not do," Maris thought, "if I just told him it was sex?"

And as she walked up to her house she saw a blur behind her curtains, and knew it was her mother's boyfriend, whom she would not be induced to call her stepfather. And she thought the muscles in his shoulders were too well developed beneath the grey t-shirt, and she thought the shirt was rank with tired sweat from too many hours driving, and there was nothing attractive in the smell.

How could her mother find it anything but vile, she thought; and isn't it true that there are some things that no amount of affection can render attractive?

"I hate that shirt," she thought, "and the smell of it, as much as anyone has ever hated anything. If I could kill him for wearing it, I am sure that in some jail or prison, someone there, when I told them my story would say I am right. Only there," she thought. "Only there. And isn't that always the way?"

In the house the man moved from the stove to the couch, and sat heavily on the couch. Maris came in the door.

"H'lo, Maris," he said.

". . . Brendan . . ."

". . . going?"

"To my room."

"Uh huh." He made a sucking sound with his lips. She stood there in the doorway, looking at him.

"N'how's everything?" he said.

"It's fine, Brendan."

"And how's your mother?" Maris tilted her head slightly to the side and up. She turned to him. "She's fine, too." She paused, the faintest suggestion of a smirk on her lips, as she looked at him, then she walked past him, back to her room.

He asked the Doctor if he had had an infection in his nose.

"I don't know what you mean," he said.

"Well, an *infection*," Henry said.

"Did it feel bad? Does it feel bad?" the Doctor said; "Well, hell, it must feel bad, or else you wouldn't *ask* it, of course. What's the trouble?"

Henry thought about the trappers, and the books he'd read, in which they toiled in the woods all Winter, proof from cold and disease — as he put it to himself —

then returned to their wives and homes in the Spring, and then, "only then," he thought, did they allow themselves the luxury of collapse.

He pictured the heavy, hairy trappers, now sweet, actually, laid low by a cold. He told the Doctor that he felt as if his nose had been infected, in what way he could not say, but in some way surely.

"How do you know?" the Doctor said.

Henry did not want to say he could smell it, but that is what he would have to say to tell him — "I can smell it. It smells like my body's rotting, or a wound, when it goes bad." But he simply said, "It just feels as if it isn't right."

"Well, I can't see that there's much wrong with you," the Doctor said. "You stop back next time you're in town."

"All right," Henry said, and he thanked him.

Out on the street the small city seemed too busy to him, after the Village. He shook his head. "Yes. It's all relative," he thought. "On the one hand, congestion; on the other hand . . ." He thought for a moment, as he looked around, and then he settled on "convenience."

Two

Each Thursday the local paper announced the upcoming weekend's auctions; and each Thursday he asked his wife, at breakfast, to remember to pick up the paper when she shopped in town. And each week he asked her again as she got in her car.

He knew the second request made him vulnerable to her anger, but she was as likely to forget the paper as to forget that he'd already asked that morning. So, each week, he asked her twice; and, when, this Thursday, her shopping done, he found she had remembered, and had brought the paper home, he was sufficiently grateful to have to stifle an urge to thank her more than once, and, so, increase her sensitivity to the issue on the following week.

He took the paper out in the mudroom, and sat on a low bench, and turned to the auction listing.

There he found an announcement of an Estate Auction, to be held in two days, on the Saturday upcoming, in a town not thirty miles off. This was a possible distance, so he read further.

He saw listed various tools, crockery, old books of stamps, various furniture, quilts, a box of medals, buttons, and badges, including the following: Cox and Roosevelt; Bryan/Free Silver; Lucky Lindy, a large badge marked "MVA," a 1948 "Minnesota Fishing and Hunting Club" patch; here he stopped reading.

What was it but the wish for treasure?

If the treasure could not be that which was recognized by all, could it not be, Henry wondered, could it not just be possible that a *private* treasure, a treasure of which only oneself knew the value, was the more precious?

"Yes," he thought, "only I know the worth."

He saw the mention of the patch, and he felt, for the moment, the Master of Time. Did it not nullify time? Yes. It did. And somewhere, he felt, he could, with the perfect talisman, sell short in 1929, before the Market fell. If he could just remember the date, of the last day of Prosperity. It was right here, and time was an illusion.

Or he could walk to safety on the *Titanic,* as the ship went down; as he knew that one side of the ship had dispatched its lifeboats only one-fourth filled — if he could but remember which side of the ship. For might he *not* be transported back there? Who could say?

Or to the Yukon, before gold was found.

And what, he wondered, would he do for funds? Would it not be ironic to be stranded in Seattle with the knowledge of Alaskan gold, and without means of buying passage?

"Yes," he thought. "But I could ... I could," he thought. "What? I could play the piano." And he reviewed the repertory which might possibly divert an 1890's boomtown crowd, and found nothing to suit. "Except," he thought, "a popular, or 'popularized' Chopin, or Schubert, which might," he thought, "which might burgeon into a New Music. A New Tin Pan Alley; and wouldn't it be ironic if my fortune lay, not in the goldfields, but in the very town which I had scorned as unimportant, and was scheming to desert?

"Life," he thought. "Life is like that. We must never exploit anything. A person. Or a situation. Or a town. Even a town. For what does it mean to scorn a thing?"

He meditated on the Barbary Coast riches which had, in the end, been won by his acceptance of the town. "Exploit the gifts you *have*," he thought.

"Dropped a fork, that's 'company coming hungry.' A fork's a woman, and a knife's a man," Mrs. Bell said. She paused. "I don't know that a spoon's a child." She sat down. "And one other thing. Puzzles me. The *disposition* of the human being to be bound by habit. And I think some of those old wives' tales . . ."

"But I took out the pole, what-would-you-call-it? A *pole*, well, that's what it is. Long *crank* affair? Winch in the *awnings*. As I thought it looked like rain, which it did. Though wasn't sure, so left it. On the porch. But sheltered? Lee-side. On the porch. Leaning up there. After I'd took the awnings in. And, yes, it didn't rain. But I noticed. I *noticed*, coming in, the garden? Afternoon? That the pansies. Around the house, getting sun, I'd not noticed that they missed, I put the awnings in. Well, then. All right. I didn't want to leave the pole on the *porch* regularly. S'I got the habit — I'd crank them out, noon, before noon, b'fore lunch, save that side of the house heating up, turn the house into a furnace, long afternoon — I got the habit, go *out* there, roll 'em in, two thirty, three, two thirty, let the flowers have that Sun, Lord knows there's little enough of it.

"And I'd leave the pole, mm? Either *on* the porch, because I'd have to crank it back in two hours, you know, the evening, setting right in your eyes, when you're sittin down, or Mac saying lower the shades, well, I don't *like* to lower the shades, whole reason that we put the *awnings* in. So I'd leave the pole, on the porch, though I hated to do it, *or,* behind the door, the *kitchen,* when I'd see it, making lunch . . ."

Her friend nodded.

"Now. Every day, end of the day, I'd take the pole, the crank, you know, and put it back. Inside the closet, under the stairs. You wouldn't of seen it there, it's back there, behind the coats, out-of-season coats, the jackets, so on, up, behind the sleeping bags."

"I was reading," her friend said, "that you're not supposed, to *store* them, all rolled up, because the *fill* in them. Gets compressed."

"Well, I spose that's why Mac stores 'em draped over the pole." She paused. "Hm," she said. "Cause I was always on him, roll the damn things, put 'em away. They roll up so small, he goes *out* there, I questioned why they have to . . ."

"Uh huh," her friend said.

". . . but that's why." She paused. "*Huh.* At least I'd *think* that's why."

"Well, why else would he *do* it that way?" her friend said. "To insist on it?"

"Well, no, I can't think another reason. So you would not have seen the pole. I don't think," she said, parenthetically, "that you've ever been in that closet."

"No. I haven't."

"Well, that's where we kept it. Since we put the awnings in. And it's not a bad place, because, of course, we do not use them in the Winter. So it makes sense, if you think about it, keep it in a place where you have seasonal *things.* Except that, I found it *convenient,* I'm cranking the damn things in three times a day, to keep it handy. So I put it 'hind the door. AND EVERY NIGHT. I go through the same, 'Put, the pole, back, in, the closet.' "

"Why? You're just going, in the morning, take it, put it back beside the door."

"So on, so on. And every night, it's as if I'm *forced . . .*"

". . . put it in the closet." Her friend said.

"Well." She threw up her hands. "Well, that's right. What do you make of that?"

"That's where it stays."

"Well, yes, but you'd think it was within the power of reason to *change* it. N'when I dropped the fork, I said, 'Goddamnit, I do *not* want to believe, *because I dropped a fork,* that I'm going to have a *hungry Female Visitor . . .'* "

"I ain't *that* hungry," her friend said, and put on a thicker accent.

"... but, you know, I *did* believe it," she said. "I *did.*" And she nodded, at her friend's smile, to mark her appreciation of the jest. "And I swear, I wasn't surprised, when you walked in here. In fact, there was no difference to it, really, between what I'd felt, and if I'd been *expecting* you. How's John? *Lord* he is getting big. N'how's *Marty* doing?"

"Well, the Trooper parked with his car nose-out," Henry said to himself. As he drove by the Trooper's house he repeated the phrase that he repeated every time he drove by and saw the car.

Each time he returned to his own home, after having seen the Trooper's car, he debated parking his truck in the driveway nose-out in emulation of the Trooper. He was restrained by the fear that neighbors would feel he was posing, and, so, he always parked in the same manner — straight-in, between the house and the small barn. "Well," he thought, ending his debate with himself as it always ended, "at least I am capable of decent self-restraint, and lay no claim to attitudes and accomplishments I have not worked to possess."

He stepped down from the truck and walked to the house. He left his hunting coat and hat on the mudroom floor, and kicked off his boots and walked into the kitchen. He put on hot water for tea, and said, "I have forgotten something."

He felt in his shirt pocket for his list of things to do

in town, and, there, on the list, he saw the word "bolt." He walked back out to the mudroom. He stepped by the small puddles caused by the snow on his boots, and stooped down and picked up his tan hunting coat. He felt in the pockets, one after the other, until he found the bolt, with its new nut and washer, nestled among lint and several loose matches, and a cheap compass, all in the small patch pocket high on the front of the coat.

"Of course I would have put it there," he thought, "because they all deal with Hunting."

The "all" to which he referred — the matches and the compass, were associated with hunting in his mind, as they were remnants of the previous Fall's hunt. The compass was one of the two he always took into the woods, the matches the last of a pack taken along to the woods to boil up his noonday tea. The bolt and nut were part of the Hunting group, as he'd bought it for his trap machine.

The small green steel machine threw clay pigeons. Now that the snow was going out, he planned to reassemble the machine and practice trap shooting.

He'd taken it out of the greasy, thick cardboard box the night before, to oil and reassemble it, and found it one part short.

The kettle whistled. Henry thought, "Where will I put it now, so that I will remember it?" And put it on the sill over the sink, where he would see it every time he washed.

He reached a cup out of the sink, and rinsed it, and cleaned it out with his fingers and rinsed it again. He turned to the stove and tapped the spout cover of the kettle, and it stopped whistling. He took a tea bag, dropped it in the cup, and poured the water in. He switched off the stove and took his tea to the table near the window, where he sat, dunking the tea bag up and down in the hot water as he looked out toward the field.

The last of the Winter's ten cord of wood lay stacked under old corrugated roofing sheets. "They say it warms you twice," he thought, "when you cut it, and when you burn it. But it also warms me when I look at it." He heard footsteps on the stairs, and bridled, as if in disgrace, as if to escape discovery in a sentimental thought; and his mind searched for a comment or observation that might, as he thought, divert suspicion, as if his wife could read his thoughts.

"Down at the hardware store," he said, as she came in the room.

She nodded. "Yes? What?"

"Hardware store."

She went to the stove, switched it on, and took the kettle to the sink and started filling it.

". . . things down there?" she said.

"Well, I'll tell you," he said, and he searched for an opinion.

"*Dickie* . . ." he said.

". . . yes?"

"I don't know how he's *doing*. . . ." He paused. "But he seems well; and I think that he's going to make it. If he'll just hang on."

"What choice does he have?" she said.

"Well, that's right."

She nodded, and she took the kettle off the stove.

She came over and sat by the window, and took out and lit a cigarette.

They both faced out, as they usually did — looking toward the field, past the woodpile, down to the pond.

"Looks like the wood'll last the Winter out," he said.

She drew on her cigarette. "Um hmm," she said.

"Well . . ." he said, and got up, and walked out to the mudroom.

As he came through the woods he felt that he was coming home.

Off to the one side of the path were the vast blocks, tumbled down the mountain. White, grey granite blocks, the color of old powder, of the old ashen tooth powder his grandfather had used.

"And in the Old Days they used the ashes themselves," Marty thought, "or salt. Nothing wrong with salt. Or ashes to clean the knives. You never find a better thing to scour with."

The path closed overhead, he jogged to the right, and then, in a while, he was at the quarry.

It loomed up on three sides of the pond. Two hundred feet. Slag and blocks, stone refuse tumbled like huge children's alphabet blocks, down into the water.

"And the trees on top," he thought. " 'F I were an Indian — but, of course, back in those days, there was no quarry here."

He climbed out onto the huge blocks. Some showing their sharp edge to the sky, all tumbled in the water. He worked his way carefully over them, out just before the pond's edge, to his favorite spot, sheltered in the angle of three of the blocks. He sat down into it and looked around.

"In a cleft of the rock," he thought, and, "Then the Lord shielded him with His hand," and he laughed softly and shook his head, as if to discount or disavow a grandiose comparison.

"Or a sniper," he thought, "certainly. Belly down, up on the crest, up there. Well, you've got to allow for the outrageous downward angle, you would have to hold so *low*; and, then, if you were *worried* by it, you've got the bad background — the water and the rock, and the water's worse than the rock anyway, though, perhaps, not at that vicious high angle." He shrugged, as if it were a moderately diverting problem for another day.

He hunched the jacket around his shoulders. "That's some Man's Work, quarrying," he thought. "What is there compares to it anymore? They make out the truck driver, and I suppose that he works hard but, what is romantic in it escapes me." He shook his head.

". . . the *Service* . . ." His mind searched for other examples of Man's Work, and his eyes swept the quarry, softly and slowly.

"One thing at a time," he said to himself. "No crow, no cat, no hawk, no anything. Nothing in the rocks, Nothing in the sky. I could sleep here.

"No. The Habits of our Youth," he thought; "And you bring the child up in the way, when he's *young* . . ." He yawned. "And in his age he will not *depart* from it." He yawned again.

"How *could* he?" he thought. He hugged his arms

close to him, and was pleased with the jacket's warmth.
Then he was asleep, and his grandfather's tooth powder
was on his palm. He saw the old man take his own
toothbrush out of the water glass, and moisten it beneath the faucet. He looked over at Marty. He scraped
his toothbrush through the powder in his palm, and
Marty did the same.

"Like a desert of camels," he thought, "in the sand."
The powder tasted of clove. It was gritty, and Marty
felt mature and sophisticated because of the taste. He
felt that his arms had grown strong, and that he was
clean, as if he'd been working hard, and sweating, and
had sweated it out, and bathed, and clothed himself in
soft fabrics to sit on the verandah and breathe in the
fields. "The scent of the fields," he thought. "Or of
Arabia, or Sand. Or Spices. Cold, like . . . cold like. Well,
good," he thought, "I'm awake. And I'm cold. I don't
have to look at my watch, for I know it is . . ." And he
debated, in his mind, between 4:05, and 4:10, and 3:55,
and 4:20.

"I don't think it is 4:05," he thought, "because that
doesn't *feel* right. It could be 4:10, though I lean toward
4:20, but that may just be because it is the outermost
time, I suppose. Or 3:55, though I definitely feel, I think,
that it is past four o'clock; so perhaps my mind has sup-
plied that early time just to give me some *balance,* so I
should think it is 4:10.

"I think that it is 4:10," he thought. "Which should
mean that I've had a good rest. And I'm nice and cold.
Good. Oh, and hasn't the *light* changed? It would be
blue, if there were color to it. Or brown. Oh, yes, and

the little snow frosting it. There's nothing in those rocks. Nothing there. Patterns, as they fall.

" 'They lay as they fell,' " he thought, and took a deep breath. He took the pack of cigarettes from a chest pocket of his jacket, and leaned into the rock to light one, cupping the cigarette and match to keep both the light and the sound contained. He smoked. After a minute he took the match head between his forefinger and thumb. Satisfied it was cold, he dropped it into his pocket.

"Why would a man want to leave?" he thought. "I am not hungry, I am reasonably warm, and . . ." He paused, in his thoughts, the pause signifying *finally,* ". . . here I *am,*" he thought.

The wind rushed through the trees on the ridge over the quarry.

"Cold up *there,*" he thought. "And it must look cold here, too, from that vantage. Water, leaden, no cheer in it, grey rocks . . ."

He knew that he had to go, and he fought the urge to stay.

"To accomplish *what?*" he thought. "And for how long? What is a minute? Or a day?

"Oh, God, I could just explode," he thought, "it's so fucken beautiful."

Back on the path he moved slowly. The wind *whisht* now and again through the trees. He walked with his hands in the jacket pockets, stepping lightly over the stones in the path. Coming up the hill, back to the road, he saw the cigarette pack. Under the birch log.

"Why didn't I see that on the way down?" he

thought, though he knew he couldn't have. For coming down the hill the pack would have been shielded from his view by the log.

He moved the log with his toe, and bent and picked the paper up. "Well, it's wet," he thought, "and it's old. And *faded,* and it's probably some *kid's.* But time was . . ."

He put it into his jacket pocket. "Time was, only people *came* up here, was us n'our friends. Not so *long* ago," he thought. And he thought of a girl in the summertime, and swimming naked in there, when what had there been better in the world than that girl swimming naked. And he thought back to his climbing the rock face, and the time he'd gotten up there, two hundred feet up, and could not get down, frozen, just below the top of the cliff, and couldn't get a grip, over, on the grass, or a root, to pull himself up, and couldn't find the projection, to start his way down, eviscerated by fear, until he had forced himself into a state of balance sufficient to start him down the cliff.

"No one will *help* you," he thought, "if you do not help yourself; and, when we're meant to *die* . . ."

The green wrecker looked black by the side of the road. He pulled himself into the cab, and, finding no reason not to start up, and drive home, he started the motor. "No, we have to warm up for a second," he thought.

"Eel legs," he thought. "That's how I thought of her. All slick from that limestone in the quarry water."

He chuckled, and was surprised to find he had a small, sly, unaccustomed grin on his face.

"Si'in' around naked. Smoking cigarettes. Her and me." His eyes went far away. "Eel legs," he thought. "Ge'en out of school. *Summer*."

Then he took a breath. And he composed himself, slowly. Granting himself the indulgence. And then he put the truck in gear, put it into a U-turn, pulled the lights on, and slowly drove away.

Three

There were twenty or thirty cars already parked up on the shoulder of the old dirt road. More were arriving as Henry walked to the auction tent. He found a spot near the back, and opened his lawnchair, and draped his tan hunting coat over the back.

There was a coffee truck, sponsored by some local Church. He walked up to the truck.

A fat fellow in an apron smiled at him.

"Yessir?"

"Oh," he said, "cuppa coffee, and — these donuts fresh?"

"Sure, they're fresh," the man said, "what do you think?"

"Yes, I'm sure they're fresh, too," Henry said. "What I meant, are they *homemade?*"

The man handed him the coffee in a Styrofoam cup.

"Milk and cream and sugar over there," he said. "*Homemade?* Where you going to find a homemade donut?" Then he laughed. "Yes. They *are* homemade, friend."

Henry took his coffee down from the truck's service window, and was adding milk to it.

"Y'want one?" the man said.

"I do," Henry said, and took the coffee and the greasy donut in a small wax-paper square, and he took his change, the coins in the palm of his hand, his fingers cupped above them holding the steaming coffee cup.

His other hand held the donut in the wax-paper square. He debated a moment about putting the donut into the pocket of his shirt, and decided that, no, the grease would bleed through. He walked back through the filling auction tent.

He sat in the lawnchair, and maneuvered the coffee cup onto the uneven ground, and balanced it there, grinding it down slightly into the earth, to make a depression. He poured his change into his shirt pocket.

The sun was burning off the morning fog. He took his glasses off and reached behind and took his sunglasses out of the pocket of his coat, and exchanged the one pair for the other.

He leaned back. He took the auction notice, ripped from the newspaper, from the pocket of his shirt, and studied it. But his thoughts were not on the inventory of the sale.

He thought: "This moment is perfect. I have my dark glasses on, and I am reading. I belong here, as anyone can see, and no one will interrupt me. I have my coffee, and it's from a fresh pot, as I got here early. I have a homemade donut. I have cigarettes in the side pocket of my coat. I have a bandanna to wipe off my hands. The day is not too warm, and there is a breeze."

He thought of the Greek who'd thrown himself into the Aegean Sea, because of "the beauty of it all."

Henry nodded at the auction inventory, and replaced it in his shirt. He took a sip of coffee. He lit a cigarette.

The tent was filling. He looked down at his watch. The auction was to start in one-half hour. Henry reached behind him, to the right hand pocket of his coat. He took out a paperback novel. He took a long breath. He closed his eyes for a moment. He exhaled, and started reading the book.

The birch trees fluttered their leaves, as if to say, "Oh, no."

Lynn pushed the white top rail of the fence back in place, and walked into the graveyard. There were the small, rusty standards, with the five-point star, "Grand Army of the Republic"; there were the old slate headstones, black and deep grey, the stone alive as an animal. These were the oldest stones, marking the graves of those who died in the early 1800s, the earliest settlers of the Village.

Lynn walked past the slim slabs of slate and soft black marble, past the heavy granite monuments, the solid Victorian markers of that age, past a stone, here and there, of someone he had known, past the markers of their parents.

Almost all of the family names were known to him. They still lived in the Village, though, since the War, they'd favored the new cemetery, twenty miles off, in town.

But this was the place, Lynn thought, the Old Graveyard; walk down the road, either way, the old dirt road, you'd see it was unchanged, the last two hundred years. Same houses, same road.

The huge sugar maples, now, along the road edge of the graveyard, they'd be a hundred, a hundred-fifty years old. Someone, back then, buried someone here, a loved one, certainly; and stood and looked, Lynn thought, and saw, in his mind's eye, the sugar maples, and felt he'd put them here.

"And here they are," he thought, "and I appreciate it."

He walked to the far edge of the little plot, and stood before the grave. He wondered, as he always did, whether to take off his hat. And he thought, "No, it wouldn't be a sacrilege, but it wouldn't be right, to perform an artificial courtesy. We were straightforward. All our life together; and she never did a thing that wasn't frank and simple and pure; and, sinner than I am, I always felt a little grace for my attempts to live up to her."

As he stood there a while, his mind quieted, as it always did; and the attempts to find meaning or ritual stopped.

The side opposite the road was fenced with a wire fence. Where it turned the corner there was a thick post, and the grave was in the corner near the post, and Lynn walked to it, and lowered himself to the ground, his back against the post. "Getting old," he thought. He looked down at the pond beyond the graveyard. "How many deer have I seen down there?" he thought. He sighed and looked back at the grave, and at the space beyond it, which would, one day, hold him.

"Yes, It's a beautiful resting spot," he thought, "The most beautiful spot I know."

The wind gusted across his face. He looked down to see the wind brushing the grass in the field, and rippling the water in the pond.

"Lots of deer," he thought.

His mind went back to the kitchen of their home, and mornings he was going hunting, and her making the coffee. He glanced back to the grave. He closed his eyes and breathed in the perfect air. He felt himself getting drowsy.

No, there were eight on the one side, and eight on the other, and these were the things he could do with them:

He could see them as alternating horizontal rows, white-black, white-black over black-white, with the white to predominate, or with the black. And he could march them that way.

Or he could march them up on the diagonal, low left to high right; first the black, in diamonds, marching up. And then the white, run them right up the diagonal, as he commanded them. And then back again, if he so desired it.

He searched for a fourth formation, and saw empty crosses, six squares formed around a hollow center, black, if the squares were white, a cross of six white squares around a black center. They guarded it, but they were vulnerable at the points of meeting, for there was just the point, just the infinite point, which, finally, was no point at all, and consisted only in the disposition of the mind to join them — just the point where the white squares on the cross joined or did not join, depending on your philosophy and mood.

And, vulnerable, just beyond that point, was the center. A black center if the cross was white.

Then he saw an illusion. The crosses arrayed, for an instant, in perspective, one behind the shoulder of the other, as if Crusaders, stretched out into the depth of the board.

"Serried ranks," he thought. "Crusaders, marching to the Holy Land. All we see are their shields."

He envisioned an intricate design of crosses-at-the-tip-of-crosses. "Like the Priest," he thought, "in some hot-climate land, where the forms have become endlessly elaborated. Where the sign of shriving grew from a cross to a cross-within-a-cross, to . . ." Then the board resolved, once more, into a mere checkerboard. As he saw the frame, the rough-wooden frame, casually screwed into the square piece of pine, which was scored into a game board. And his mind came back to the voice of the auctioneer, hawking something.

"Was I asleep?" Henry thought. "Or was I hypnotized? Did I lapse into some Hindu State of Consciousness? Or did I drift away? What was I thinking of?

"Many times, when you are asleep, there is no line between it and waking, and the thoughts that you have meld. In their own reason — so satisfying. So full. So renewing. Like heat, or a perfect day, when there is just the right sun on you. On the back porch, say, and the equilibrium of sun and breeze, so that you couldn't say if you were warm or cool, so that you couldn't say."

". . . and five, and five, and now *Forty*," the auctioneer said. "Now Forty. *Yes*. Now Five." He looked around. "*Five? Five?* Yes. I see you. Yes, ma'am . . . you are . . . Yes, ma'am, you are Forty. I have for . . . *Five? Yes!* And now Fifty. Fifty, where? I have Forty-five. *Fifty . . . ? Fifty?*" He paused. He looked around, as his two helpers scanned the crowd for bids. "All in? All done? . . . *Fifty . . . ? Fifty . . . ?*" It hung in the air. And the crowd waited. There was no "going Once . . ." It was the auctioneer's pleasure to extend or stop the bidding at will.

". . . and Fifty . . . ?"

"*Yuh!*" one of the spotters said.

"Now Fifty-five," the auctioneer said. "Fifty-*Five. Yes!* Now *Sixty . . .*"

The Banker said that he required various years of Dick's records, so he gathered them and boxed them. He tied the box closed with string. He went to the kindling box by the woodstove and fished out a large brown paper bag. He tore the bag open and laid it flat, and laid the string-wrapped box on it. He opened the drawer of his desk and took a spool of thick strapping tape, and found the tape nearly gone. He sighed, and got up heavily, and walked downstairs into the store.

Down in the store he found he was out of the strapping tape, and went next door to the food store.

"Afternoon, *Dick*," Gary said.

"Gary."

"How is zit with *Dick* this afternoon?" Gary said.

"Well . . ." Dick said. He walked down the aisle to the small display of school supplies.

". . . help you with?" Gary said.

"Looking for *strapping* tape."

"Y'ain't got it chure place?" Gary said.

"Out of it," Dick said.

"Well, I'nn know . . ." Gary said. "I. Don't. Know. B'lieve that I should have some." He came down the aisle.

"I'll find it," Dick said.

"Yep. Oh, no. No question of that," Gary said, coming down the aisle. "B't the Farmer's *Boot* . . ." He nodded at Dick. ". . . eh?" Dick looked at him. ". . . is the best *manure.*"

"He looks like he was born with his face washed," Dick thought.

"Here we got it," Gary said. He reached past Dick, and picked the roll off the shelf, and handed it to him.

Dick took the tape, and started back up the aisle. He looked back and saw Gary had taken a pencil and a small spiral notebook from his jacket and was making notes, looking at the shelf.

Dick waited by the cash register till Gary came back.

Gary took the roll of tape. "Two ninety-nine, and some for the *Governor,* is three *sixteen,* and what *else* can we do for you today?" Dick smiled.

"That it?" Gary said.

"Yes, Gary. That's about it." He handed him four

dollar bills, and took his change, and left the store. He ran through the rain the twenty yards back to the hardware store, hunching his shoulders.

"I run like an old man," he thought. "I run like I'm fat. Like I'm fat and old."

Back on his stool in the store he took the big yellow bandanna from his back pocket and rubbed his head something like dry. He spread the bandanna on the counter in front of him, half on the top, and half hanging off the counterfront, to dry. He opened the roll of tape, and began to wrap his financial records.

And one time he'd talked to Gary, when Gary had only owned the farm stand, down the road, and Gary told him he was buying the food store, too, and Dick told him that that was a rough business, and Gary shrugged. In the next year, when the food store was, for the first time in anyone's memory, a success, Dick had asked Gary where he got the expertise; and Gary said he'd never done it before in his life, but he figured anything that another man could do, that he, Gary, could do, and what could it be, beyond common sense?

The ass-end of the school bus stuck out of the garage. The rain beat on its roof. And when they were not working, they could hear it up by the hood, up in the garage. Marty was working on the engine, and his son, John, sat at the counter, on the metal stool, supposedly engaged in his schoolwork, but listening to the men; and they knew he was listening, and did not care.

Marty came out of the engine, and sighed, straightening up. ". . . the monkeys," Carl said.

". . . uh, yuh, the monkeys," Marty said, softly, as he walked to the counter. He held his finger up, as a sign, to Carl, who stayed back at the bus: No. I haven't forgotten.

John started to get up, and Marty motioned him to keep his seat. He reached past his son, to a drawer in the counter, and took out a calculator, black with grease. He wiped his hands on a rag from his back pocket. He stared at the calculator for a moment, then began punching numbers into it. He stopped, and looked at his son vacantly, until he noticed the boy thought he wanted something from him. Then he shook his head, and started writing numbers on a receipt pad.

Carl walked to the front of the garage, and stood by the school bus, just inside the rain, looking out.

"What's five times nine?" Marty said to his son. "Forty-five," the boy said, and Marty shook his head, and wrote another number on the receipt pad.

Carl stood in the doorway, smoking his short cigar. Across the street he could see Dick, at his desk in the hardware store, and the sign "Douglas Hardware," swinging in the rain. "Spring rain . . ." Carl thought, "and the potbellied stove." He shrugged, and ran his tongue around his teeth, as if to say, "Some people find a worth in that."

"Half of the purpose of a thing . . ." he said to himself, and was startled by the whir of an air-wrench. He strolled back along the bus, where Marty stood, on a small, battered metal step, body half-in, half-out of the hood of the bus. He glanced over at the boy, who lowered his head to his book.

Marty came out of the hood. He balanced the wrench on the nose of the bus, and patted his pockets. He took the receipt pad from the front of the leg pocket of his coveralls, and made a note on it.

"Just like a whorehouse," Carl said.

". . . d'y' mean?" Marty said.

"Y'ever been in a whorehouse?"

Marty looked at him, then swiveled his head slightly, to include the boy. Carl grinned, as if to say, "*I* know he's there . . ."

"In a *whorehouse*," he began, elaborately indicating that his speech was a lesson geared down for the uninitiated. "In a *whorehouse*, whore comes in, y'choose her, or, whatever, if y'got to take what you get; n'you *tell* her, mm? You go to her *cubby*, n'you *tell* her what it is you *want*, n'she goes *away*." Marty craned his neck side-to-side, to relieve the stiffness. He took the rag and wiped his hands. He sighed, and sat on the bumper of the bus. Carl sat by him.

"N'*then* . . ." he said, elaborately not including the boy in his speech, "they *stay* away awhile, n'y'r wondering: 'Th'hell are they *doing*?' or 'Is it just *me* . . . ?' N'then they come back, and . . . but *later*, mmm? Y'r wondering: 'Where did they *go*, what were they *doin'*, for the love of Christ?'" He made an appeal to Marty. "What could they've been doin'?"

"Hell," Marty said. "*I* don't know . . ."

"N'how the hell *long*, t'h'out this *scribbling*, so on, till I get the bus back?"

Marty smiled. "What do *you* think . . . ?" He called to his son. "*John*. Mister *Charles*, wants to know, 'n he gets his bus back."

The boy lifted his head from his book. "He can have it right now, if he doesn't care if it runs or not," he said. Marty shrugged at Carl, to say, "Then what can I do . . . ?"

Marty took out a cigarette, and lit it, and smoked it, resting on the bumper. He and Carl sat there, smoking. After a bit Carl nodded. They sat there a while more. "Well," Marty said, as if the word were in quotes. Carl turned slightly toward him. "Around the position. We did not know they were monkeys, we heard this 'jabber,' what were you goin' to think?"

"Language," Carl said. Marty raised his hands, to say, "Well, what would *anyone* think?"

"N'any case," he said, speaking quite softly, "there was a f'nn *million* of 'em, by the sound, and you think . . ." He gestured to Carl, who acknowledged him. "N' 'I should of fucked that girl that time . . .' " Carl nodded, again, sedately.

"Well, we're pourin' it *in* to 'em, and we're on the *radio,* but, like I said . . ." He gestured outside, at the rain, and Carl nodded again.

"N'so, it's 'Shut up and die like an Infantryman.' *Daybreak* . . ." he said, "we're still here. 'What in the History of *Time?*' " Carl began to form his face into a chuckle. "N'out we go, and two hundred *rock*-apes, *Land*-apes . . ." He shrugged it off. ". . . they told me, out-for-the-count."

"Monkeys," Carl said.

"I hope to tell you." Marty walked to the front of the garage, and flicked the cigarette out in the rain. He came back toward the hood. "Sounded more human, many folks we *know*," he said, and stepped back on his stool, and put his head back under the hood.

It became quiet in the garage, save for the rain on the roof of the bus. The boy heard the scratching of his pencil, and Carl, who would clear his throat now and again. The boy chanced a glance at Carl, to see if he was being watched, but the man's eyes were focused far away.

John tried purposefully to catch the man's glance, but Carl took no notice of him. Then John lowered his head to his book, and found, after a while, that he had begun doing his schoolwork.

The Trooper walked up to the house, out of the path of the porch light. His boots made a squelching sound in the dew-heavy grass.

He kept his eyes on the front door. Forty-five feet short of it he swung wide, to catch a glimpse, if possible, through the side window of the cabin. But the window was curtained. All that he saw was butter-yellow light, and no shapes moving beyond it.

Still in the dark, he turned back and surveyed the woods. He saw no movement there. Just the dirt road, and his cruiser parked on it.

He walked up on the porch, and stood to one side of the door and knocked. "State Police," he said.

He waited a moment, and was about to knock again, when the door was opened by a woman in her forties.

Her fat face was slack with liquor. She had a large, purple bruise on her left temple. "Mrs. Barnes?" he said. She looked at him.

"Your husband here?" She didn't respond, and he moved closer to the door, trying to get a look inside. "Is your husband here?" he said.

"He ain't here."

"Uh huh," then, "Could I come in, please?" He cast a glance back at the road, then moved quickly past her into the cabin.

He was in the main room. There was a wood cookstove, and a sink with a pump in it, a dining-room table, and various rough-wood shelves holding food. There was a plastic gun rack on the wall, with space for two rifles. The bottom tier held a cheap fishing rod, and the top tier was empty.

There was a rough, plasterboard partition, and in the room beyond it he saw the foot of a bed, and rumpled bedclothes bunched next to it, on the floor.

"You mind closing the door?" he said. He looked quickly behind him as she did so, and while she was turned away he unsnapped the safety catch on his holster. He moved toward the bedroom.

"He ain't here," the woman said.

"Uh huh," the Trooper said. He felt around the doorframe, on the far side of the partition, and found the light switch on the wall. He threw the switch, but the room stayed dark.

"It's broke," she said.

He took the flashlight from his belt, and stepped into the bedroom, holding the flashlight in his left hand, high, and wide of his body, as he switched it on. He scanned the room. The light showed clothes scattered on the bed and floor, a cheap dresser with its drawers all pulled open, and one drawer missing.

The missing drawer lay on the bed, upside down. The room smelled fetid. He switched off the light.

Back in the main room the woman was seated on a low, grey sofa, smoking a cigarette. The Trooper came into the room, and stood in a corner. He took out his notebook.

"Would you tell me what happened, ma'am?" After a moment she shrugged. He took the notebook and his pen in his left hand, and looked around him, at the two windows, one opposite him, one on his left hand.

"Well, ma'am, perhaps you'd like to come into the *Shelter.*" He paused. "N'we could get you *looked* at. Shall we do that now . . . ?"

She looked up at him for the first time. "I have to swear a complaint?" she asked.

"No, ma'am, but I would advise it." She nodded.

"Waaal . . ." she said, her voice slurred from drinking, "waaal, he's gone . . ."

"Why don't you get your coat, and I'll take you down?"

She looked around the room. She pursed her lips, and shook her head, and got up awkwardly from the low, cheap sofa.

The Trooper wrote in his notebook. He turned his hand over to see his watch, and noted the time, then put the book back in the holder on his belt.

She walked to the door, and took a worn, red duffle coat from a nail, and began to put the coat on.

"He took his things, did he?" he said. She looked at him and nodded. She looked around, then walked to the table, where a grey, knit cap lay, among various dirty dishes. ". . . took his rifle, too?"

She looked at him inquisitively for a moment, then at the gun rack; and she turned back to him. She held his gaze awhile, then looked away. "Waal, yeah, he . . ." She stopped, then gestured, taking in the room, as if that were an explanation of all she wanted to say.

He moved toward the door and opened it, motioning her to go out first. As she did, he stepped back and hit the light switch by the door. The porch light went out.

"I can't see," she said.

He came out on the porch and closed the cabin door behind him.

"Do you want to lock it?"

"I can't see," she said.

"You want to lock your door?" he said.

She turned back toward him and said nothing. He took her arm, and helped her down the cabin steps.

Down the road was his cruiser. They walked toward its right side. He opened the rear door, and helped her into it, then moved quickly behind the car to the driver's side, and got in.

He started the engine.

The car moved up toward the cabin, and made a quick three-point turn and headed back down the dirt road. After a hundred yards he snapped the headlights on, and increased his speed.

Back on the blacktop he reached for the handset. The woman took a pack of cigarettes from the pocket of her coat. She held the end of the pack against her upper lip and moved it back and forth.

"Twenty-seven Alpha, Twenty-seven Alpha: I have a female victim and complainant in transit. The time is now . . ." He glanced at his dashboard clock.

Four

Dick thought of riches as he looked in the fire.

It was an old railroad stove; a potbellied stove, shaped like two cones, arranged base-to-base, forming the fat waist.

The platform on top held a coffeepot, but he didn't make coffee in it. The pot held water, to add some moisture to the dry Winter air.

But now the pot was empty. Once in a while he'd stop by the stove and look into the pot, to see the cakes, limestone flakes from the boiled-away water; and, through the Summers, he'd often find a dead fly or two, and he'd shake the fly out and replace the pot on the stove.

Coffee was made in a plastic machine on the ledge by the front of the store.

He looked from the fire toward the store front, the window, and the street. It was a cold, wet day. He walked to the ledge and poured himself a cup of coffee. He took a napkin from the dispenser, and wiped down the counter where the customers had soiled it.

He drew air through his pursed lips, and came back to the potbellied stove.

He could see the fire, red and white, through the isinglass window in the door. He reached in his left pants pocket and brought out a small pocketknife. He used the end of the knife handle to lift the nickeled knob on the door, and threw the napkin in.

He looked at the fire and thought of riches. He backed up to his chair, and sat in it, his back to the window, and looked at the fire.

Out in the shed behind the store were fifteen cord of hardwood cut and stacked, one year old. "Well," he thought; "well, *that's* wealth of a sort. And if I want to have a fire today; and if it *turns* warmer this afternoon — as it may — or, then, again, it may *not* — it was cold this morning; n'if I want to have a fire, I can *have* it. And not only do *I* appreciate it, but the customers will, too, as they come in here."

And then he was frightened, for it had been proved to him that every certainty concealed its opposite; and a goddess more wrathful and immediate than Nemesis watched for the least sign of assurance on the part of Man.

"Well, all right. Well, fine, then, I'll take it as a question," he thought; "if the customers, seeing the fire, would think me weak to have it this early; or, *Or . . .*" he thought, "if they might find it a luxury, which I'd given myself." He shook his head. "And *wouldn't, wouldn't* they just assume it was a luxury for *me,* rather than *them,*" he thought. "And even if they thought it was for them . . ." He smiled, as if to say, "There is the wisdom in it"; "Wouldn't they expect a fire *next* time on a day like this, and wouldn't they feel slighted if I didn't have one?" He nodded, thinking, "Of *course* they would . . . "Well, *hell* . . ."

He stepped to his desk, feeling the heat of the beautiful stove. He leaned behind the register, and took his pipe and pouch and tamper in one hand. He straightened up and started filling his pipe.

He smiled at the stove.

"Nothing like it," he thought.

"The *truth* of the matter is, I'm a warm son of a bitch in dry clothes in front of this very stove, smoking my pipe; and, as to what may happen tomorrow, or this afternoon, that is not ours to know; and that's the goddamn truth."

He struck a wooden match on the top of the stove, and sat on the chair near the door as he lit his pipe.

"The *God* damn truth?" he thought. "And anyone who thinks otherwise is deluded." He shook the match out.

"What is there that can't fail?" Another part of his mind began to object that the very question might alert the goddess, and it might be prudent . . . "No," he thought, speaking, as it were, to that other voice. "No, I'll *address* it, and I believe I'm free to *do* so; and if I'm not, then that will have to be as it may. *What* . . ." He thought, taking his main strain up, "is not liable to be destroyed? Or uprooted? Or . . . or . . ." He cast about for an example, and found it amusing that he'd have to do so, as such examples were the bulk, he thought, as he smiled, of his waking reflections. And he cast about for a firm base to build his argument, finding that he felt stilted, as his thoughts lapsed into the abstract.

"Well, a *dam* may break," he thought, "build it how strong we will. Or the rich man may be *kidnapped*," he thought, "or robbed. *Any* certainty may be proved false. It *is* false," he thought. "What is real?

"It is true that if *anything* is true, that I am sitting here."

He looked at the fire. He looked at the electric clock on his desk. It read: 10:07.

He rubbed the back of his neck, and sighed.

Out on the street the rain came down.

He looked out and saw Marty in the garage, working on a truck. A car went too fast down the Village street, its lights on, spraying water to either side.

He sighed. "So many things to do," he thought. "I could be —" The phone rang and startled him. He turned back from the window and stood up.

He started for the phone, then turned back, gathered his coffee cup and his smoking things, and carried them to the counter and put them by the register. He walked behind the register, and stepped up on the small platform. He picked up the phone.

"Douglas *Hardware*," he said cheerily. "Yes? Yes, I will," he said.

He sat on his stool, and reached past his pipe rest to a pack of cigarettes. He took one and lit it and drew on it.

"*Hello!*" he said. "Mr. *Breen* . . . thank you for . . . not at all," he said, and looked at the clock.

"Nope. Just the business of the day. Glad that you called."

He covered the phone with one hand. "Honey, would you help that lady with her order, please?" he said to the store.

"Mr. *Breen*," he said. "I was wondering when I might come in to —" He listened. "Well, that's —" he said. "That's what I —" He listened again.

"Well, no, sir," he said, "... an extension is *exactly* ..."

He looked up to the sound of the store door opening.

"Marge, *hello*," he said. "... 'thing you want, you let me know."

He turned back to the phone, and angled his body into the corner of the register nook, as the woman moved back through the store.

"I'm sorry ..." he said to the phone. And listened.

"You see," he said, "you, you see, that's what I'm *saying*. I believe the last *figures* you have don't adequately *represent* the, not only the *volume* of; but, if I may, the 'tone' ..."

In his rehearsing the speech he'd felt less than certain about using the word "tone" in a financial conversation, and had debated leaving it out; but now he'd said it, and he was pleased with the bluntness of the sound. "And if that cocksucker don't like it," he thought, "then he knows nothing about a business."

"Which is picking ..."

"Ten p'y nails ... ?" the woman said; and he turned and pointed back to the nail bin.

"Which is, by *your* standards ..." he said to the phone. "Picking, what? Picking *up*. By *your* ... What? I'm saying let me come *in* ... let me ... let me just ...

look, look, look, mister . . . let me. Let me come in. Man-to-man, and . . ."

He stopped, and listened. He stood.

"When, all right, when, when would be a good . . ." He scribbled a note on the pad in front of him.

"All right, I'll . . ." he said.

"Fine. That's fine. But wouldn't it be faster if I just took my charts, and . . .

"No. No," he said. "I'll be here. Yes. Fine. No. I appreciate it. *Whenever* you . . ."

The woman came up and put the small brown paper bag of nails on the counter near the register.

"All right. Fine. Fine. I appreciate it. Thank you. Thank you very much." He hung up the phone.

"Well, Marge; what have *you* got there?" he said.

He opened the bag, then put it on the small scale on the counter, and made a notation on the sales slip.

"Seventy-three cents," he said.

She nodded, and took the bag and walked toward the door.

". . . set it down . . . ?" she said.

"Sure thing," he said, and winked at her. The door closed. He sat down on the stool. He looked at the telephone, and shook his head slowly.

He took a drag on his cigarette and stubbed it out. He turned and looked out at the rain.

"The bubbles round the inside of the coffee cup," the old man said, "when they head for the cup, to make a ring around it, that's low pressure. When the Martin Farm

stands out, the silos, and you see it from the road, as if it
was clearer and larger, up against the sky; when it jumps
out and you say 'I did not *think*, all these years, it was that
close,' that's *high* pressure. And the numerous other
signs — why, I remember Charlie, could convert them,
not only into 'going to rain,' which anyone might do, but
to the habits of the animals. Which, if you think of it,
don't they respond to the same signals? Except, with
them, they are thinking, '*If* it's going to rain, then that will
affect so-and-so' (whatever they eat). 'Which is more
likely, that case, they'd be down at the *pond*,' or so on.

"Now, that's wisdom. Y'see? For *they* do not think
of it, or aren't aware of it, or I don't *think* they are.
However, they *act* on it. N'by *observing* them, now,
Charlie Taggart, n'th'Old Timers, came to know their
world."

The old man stopped and took another drag of his
cigarette.

The two boys, John, and James, stood, respectfully,
listening, at the check-out counter, James in his apron,
and John standing outside the counter itself, his six-pack
of cola in the paper bag down on the counter.

The old man looked up.

"He would say, 'Goin' up Loach Dam for pickerel,'
and we would go up there. B'fore a rain. Eh? *Get* there,
nobody had took nothing out of the lake, all that morning. Clouds coming in, f'r the North. We go out. He ups,
and I don't know, what the hell he puts on his line.
Thwap. There's your fish. Bait. He was usin' some kind of
paste. Baits up again. Thwap. 'N'other pickerel, so on.
Weather front, closing in. He musta, every pickerel in

the Lake, Looks over, like this . . ." The old man looked over his shoulder. "Reels his line in, shuts the tackle box, 'that's it.' Nobody caught a fish, b'fore or *after* we was there. N'that's a *small* thing.

"*One* time. Waay back in th'woods. The other side the mountain . . ."

John took one of the soda cans out of the paper bag. Easing it out; and opened it quietly, and took a sip.

". . . all right? Two sets'a tracks. Two sets'a tracks. I'm reluctant, hunter that *I* am, t'say it's not the same deer." He reached out toward the boys, to say, "Bear with me here." "Y'know, how they mark up an area; you'd say, you didn't know better, 'Twenty-five deer been through here.' " John nodded, with enough of a smile to show respect; "No," it was saying, "I recognize that you are not speaking to me quite as an equal. Though there is not that much of difference between that and this."

". . . but *Charlie:* nodded. Didn't even have to speak. Meaning, yep, that's two deer."

"And when I'm grown you'll be gone," John thought.

". . . z'at girl of *yours,* John?" The man said. John looked around, surprised. His friend chuckled. The old man made a face, to say, "You see, there's all *sorts* of forms, observation."

"If you start thinking too much about death — if you think about it — what is it? The fellow's dead. He used to be alive; now he's dead.

"It's the suffering, of course, that may be in those who survive him. There's no gainsaying that. But, apart from that, what does it mean? He was here, now he's not. And I can't think anything more of it than that," Carl said.

"And would you of dropped the hammer on him?" Dickie said.

"Dropped the hammer," Carl said, and he paused, and nodded minutely, as if in response to a thought he had had.

"You can't say what you would've done, of course. After the fact. 'I would of done this,' or 'I wouldn't of.' But I *believe* — or, let me put it differently — I *was ready* to kill him."

"No. I can't blame you," Dickie said.

A woman came into the store. Dickie and Carl turned their heads to her, and Carl nodded.

"Has my husband been in?"

"No, he hasn't," Dickie said, and she left, and the screen door banged behind her.

"First time I'd of killed a man. Outside the Service," Carl said. "*Well.*" He got up off the crate he was sitting on. "Guess I'll get on home," he said. "But you be careful, back the Woods."

"Believe me, I will," Dickie said.

"And ain't just the French *Canadians.*"

"No."

". . . and it may not be *primarily* them."

"But *these* guys were . . . ?"

"I hope to tell you," Carl said.

"What, you told it by their *accent?*"

"Well, that would do it," Carl said.

"Uh huh."

"And, also, they dress differently."

"Uh huh."

"You tend to notice that, you know. The things you see."

"Moments of stress. Yes," Dickie said. The door banged.

"Lynn, come over here," Dickie said; and the farmer came to the counter. "Tell him what you told me."

Carl, about to leave the store, paused, and came back to the counter, and he looked at the two men. Then he told his story again.

The story took place during the previous deer season. In it Carl was walking in the woods, Still Hunting. He was following a buck he'd patterned in the months before.

Carl followed the tracks and saw that the buck, true to his habits, had risen from his bed and walked down and drunk at the stream. He had then returned up the mountain to a dense area of blow-down, and, in the middle of the day, had rested.

As the buck rested, Carl decided to do the same. He leaned his rifle up against a tree, and sat down, some four feet away, with his back against another; and, as he said, he "must of fell asleep."

When he woke, he said, there were four men, hunters, standing some ten feet away and looking at him.

As Carl spoke, Henry walked into the shop. He saw in the postures of the men that a serious and therefore private tale was being told. He closed the screen door quietly, and eased himself into the corner, where he listened.

"And they were just *staring* at me. And I woke up. I can't think why they're just *standing* there, except I'd *felt* them, somehow, and my waking up had stopped them, what they's going to do."

"And there was no one behind you," Dickie said.

"No," Carl said, "that's right. I can't say how I knew. But I was certain. That was all of them."

"And we looked at each other. No one moved, it seemed, for a long time. And then the *leader* of 'em said, 'That's a nice rifle.' " Carl paused.

"Now. When I say those words to you, it's *impossible* to convey the feeling he gave me. But I *knew* ..." Lynn, the farmer, nodded; and Carl looked at him, as if to say, "That's right, it was as plain as day."

The store was silent. Dick cleared his throat. Quietly.

"The men spread out. *So* slightly," Carl said. "Or, perhaps, if you'll bear with me, it was as if I could sense their *intention*. Old guy. Looking at my rifle. Four feet away. I'm flat on the ground. Midst of the woods. I'm thinking, 'Son of a bitch. One of us is going to die.' "

There was a shadow, from the window, and everyone in the store glanced that way. Henry, in the corner, thought, "Oh, please. No one come in the store now." On the sidewalk, the woman walked past the store; and the men looked back, toward each other, ignoring Henry, and all understood that he had neither been included nor overlooked, but that his respectful silence had entitled him to temporary status as a third thing, which is to say, as someone who neither was nor was not in the store.

"Because," Carl said, "because the man *started* to move, do you see, towards the rifle, and the other one, next to the outside, on the left, he took a glance toward the old man, and then he started in toward me." Carl paused, and shook his head. His lips formed into a small frown.

"Started in toward me," he said. "Well. I let my coat fall open. And I *Thank God* I hadn't buttoned it up, because if I had, I'm sure as my hope of Salvation that I'd be dead now.

"I let my coat fall open, and they saw the glimpse of the grips of my belt gun. And the young one stopped. And then the old one stopped.

" 'That's right,' I thought, 'You son of a bitch. You son of a *bitch*. You want to motherfucking bushwack a man, his own *woods?*' And the old man stopped. And he looked at me."

"How many could you take?" Dick said.

"I couldn't tell you that. I don't know that I could of took *one*."

"Oh, come *on* . . ." Dick said.

"I'm on the *ground*. Got to draw *cross*-draw. Shoot *up* . . . I don't know, scared as I was, Dick, I could of hit a goddamn thing." He paused. ". . . I *think* I could."

"Which were you going to shoot?" said Lynn. "The old one?"

"Well, that's right. I'm going to go for him *first,* as it seems, he's the only one *knows* anything . . ."

". . . uh huh," Lynn said.

"In *any* case," Carl said, "they stopped. The old one said something in French. And they walked off. Careful. Backing up. A bit, and then they turned around. Nice as you please. And went back in the woods."

And that was the end of the story. The listeners felt as if they had let out a breath; and, slowly, in respect for the mood, they began to rearrange themselves.

Dick got down off his stool and poured himself a cup from the coffeepot.

"Waaaaaallllp," Lynn said, and moved back into the store, on the errand that had brought him there.

"Yessir," Dick said. "*Do* for you, Hank . . . ?"

The girl sat in the cold room. Up against the headboard, with her legs under her. She saw glimpses of the man, as he moved in the bathroom. She saw him reflected in the mirror over the sink, and, again, in that on the door.

"His suit is blue," she thought, "and no one wears that blue a suit. It's blue like the only blue you see in that kind of suit. It *Don't* oc*cur* in *Na*ture," she thought. She beat her right hand on the chenille bedspread, in time to her litany.

"Although you could lay in the tub, and lay there," she thought, "and angle the mirrors so that you could watch the television *while* you were in the tub. Not only would that divert you, but the reflection, having been done twice, would turn the image right-side-round again. As if that made a difference."

As she thought, she found she was disappointed, and

that the image so corrected robbed her of a legitimate and accidental novelty.

"If it was reversed you could watch for any *humor* that might arise from it," she thought; "whatever *that* might be." She repeated the last thought to herself: "Whatever that might be."

"That man does not know," she thought, "that I can see him as he putters about. Or, if he does, he is less or maybe more interesting than I'd given him credit for, *although* I do not care."

But then he was coming out of the bathroom, with his sport coat and pants on his arm, and he walked to the bureau to put them down, avoiding her eyes.

She looked at him as he passed, and saw the white card on the back of the door. "An Act for the Protection of Innkeepers," she read.

" 'This Act,' " she began, " 'shall be construed . . .' "

". . . any time . . . ?" she heard him say. She turned to him.

"What?" she said.

". . . to be *home* any time?" he repeated.

"Do I Have To Be Home Any Time," she said to him, beating the time of the sentence out with her right hand on the bed. "And I don't even know what I *mean*," she thought; "but let *him* figure that out." Her eyes glazed for a moment.

"Let him supply it," she thought. "For what does it mean, *anyway*? Or if they say that Britain and France '. . . had been bitter rivals'? What the hell other kind of rivals you find? All the rules," she thought. "*Bullshit*. Someone *gets* there, n'then they want to pull the *ladder* up. Huh. 'They were Bitter Rivals.' " She sniggered. "Idiots . . ." The man turned.

"Well, all right," she thought, looking at him, "whatever you want to *make* of it."

The truck would not move. It crept along at twenty-five miles an hour. He saw the earth loaded high above its sides, and the huge, filthy tailgate before him — two monstrous chains hung down, one from each corner of the tailgate, and that was his view.

There was no place to pass, he knew, for twenty miles; and he could take a chance, and pull out past the truck, but on this mountain road it could be suicide.

"Son of a bitch, pull over, or slow down and wave me by," he thought. But the truckdriver did neither, and the two crawled along. He turned the radio on. All he heard was static, and he cut it off.

The chains, dancing almost in unison, drew his attention — two six- or eight-foot lengths of heavy chain, links as thick as a man's wrist; and he reflected that he probably could not lift the chain if he had to.

A heavy, greasy chain. He watched it shake. "It shakes," he thought, "like a black dancer. From the waist down. Where it fastened to the tailgate, at the top, that is the waist. And the chain is the body of the world's greatest black dancer. Dancing the slowest possible dance.

"As if we were in Paris," he thought; and, "wouldn't that show me some fucking." He looked at the chain.

"White people couldn't dance that good. Who are

we kidding?" It shook itself down and snaked with a regular, and, at once, a varied rhythm. "Into the ground," he thought. "All that weight. Shaking down." "There is no tune," he thought. "*That* is the tune. It comes from the hips down. And shakes it off itself, and starts in its own good time. There it is.

"Like the world's greatest lover. Yes," he thought. "She is. In some Bistro in Paris. What does *she* care? That's why the people go there. To see the dance. It's from another culture."

He watched what he'd come to think of as his chain. Keeping his distance, two car-length back from the truck, both of them moving at twenty-five miles an hour on the winding road.

He saw the sign "Stop and Eat," and the gravel parking lot, and looked to his right at the diner as he drove past it.

He continued down the road, after the truck, for some hundred yards, then glanced in the rearview mirror, and did a tearing U-turn.

In the diner two men at the counter looked up and behind them. They saw the car as it completed the turn, and came back down the road and onto the gravel in front of the diner.

Henry got out of the car.

The men at the diner looked at him through the glass for the briefest moment, then turned back to the counter, one after the other.

"Waal, the shit kicked out of *her*, I want to tell you," the one said. The other nodded.

"The dispensary, the bruises up and down her *back*,

the hell he's beatin' on her with *escapes* me; why, she . . ."

The two men looked over their shoulders to the door, as they heard it open. ". . . why she put *up* with it," the man concluded.

Henry walked to the far end of the counter. Far enough not to seem to intrude; not, he thought, so far as to give the impression that he found the men odious. And he sat down.

There were small, rectangular menus, encased in plastic, in an old, tin holder on the counter. He picked one up, and read on it "Breakfast."

"This the Breakfast Menu, that you're serving now?" he said.

The man farthest from him got up and walked back behind the counter. "Is that the *breakfast* menu . . . ?" the man said.

". . . you *serving* breakfast now . . . ?" Henry said. He held the menu toward the man. "My question is, what is the *menu* that you've got on now?"

"Holding it," the man said.

Henry bobbed his head. "Could I get a cup of coffee?" he said. The man turned back to a coffee urn. Henry looked around.

There were several cardboard signs, with the usual sayings, up on the wall over the grill. And, above them, two old, single-shot .22 rifles, each with an index card beneath it, with the model name elaborately done in pencil in an attempt to resemble German black letter. The larger of the two, Henry saw, was *The Stevens Favorite*, and the smaller *The Little Scout*.

Off at the end of the diner, out of the light, was a
glass-fronted case with various pistols in it. Above it was
a cheap, stenciled sign, reading, "Guns for Sale."

The man brought the coffee, and Henry turned back
to him. "Could I get an order of toast?" he said. The
man looked at him, and he changed the focus in his eyes,
and narrowed them, Henry thought, as if there were
something to wonder at in the request. And then he nodded, and went back to the back counter. He took two
slices of bread from a white, unlabeled package, and
dropped them into a large toaster.

". . . why she would *let* him do it," the other man at
the counter said.

"Y'know the answer to that well as me," the owner
said, without turning back. He took a white, chipped
navy mug from a rack, and drew himself a cup of coffee;
and came and leant, with his forearms on the counter,
near his friend. He reached toward him and took a pack
of cigarettes out of the pocket of his shirt, brushing the
other man's jacket aside to get it.

He took a cigarette and replaced the pack in his
friend's pocket.

"That *cocksucker*. Found the *button*. That *drives*
that girl," he said. He tapped the cigarette on the coun-
tertop to emphasize his words. ". . . and then he *pushed*
it," he said.

Henry took his coffee cup and walked down the
counter toward the guncase, away from the men. The
customer at the counter looked up at him. The owner
did not. He lit his cigarette and stood.

"He pushed it, and she got everything she always

wisht for." He paused. "Be *abused* . . ." he said, and took
a drag on his cigarette. "State *Troopers* . . ." he began.
The *thut* of the toaster stopped his speaking. He raised
one index finger, infinitesimally, toward his friend, and
the other man nodded.

He moved back to the toaster, and took the toast
and buttered it with a large, black-bladed knife. He took
a heavy white plate from a rack at eye level, and used the
knife to slide the toast onto it.

He took the plate to the counter, to the place where
Henry had been sitting.

Henry turned and walked back quickly, as the man
put down the plate. He inclined his head toward the
case. "You sell guns here?" he said.

". . . State *Residents* . . ." the man said.

"Well, yes. I am," Henry said. The man walked back
down the counter.

". . . prove it?" he said. "Yes. I can," Henry said.

The man looked at him for a moment, bit his lower
lip, and let it drag itself out slowly from behind his
teeth.

"Ayuh. We sell 'em," he said. He cleared his throat,
and he leaned back against the counter.

"In *Jesus'* name we ask it."

His wife looked around the table, and the children
began to eat.

"mmmm . . . *Central* . . . ?" Marty said.

The boy, his mouth full, shook his head, to say,
"N'moment."

"Things g'ng with the County contract?" his wife said.

The boy looked at his father. "Game? Piece cake," he said.

Marty smiled. "Y'r sure that you want to say that b'fore the Game?"

"You *ast* him . . ." his wife said.

The boy shrugged and grinned.

"How are we doing with the . . . ?"

"County's going fine," Marty said.

"You said there might be some difficulty with the bid."

"The bid, no," he said. "*You* seein' *Judy* to-night . . . ?"

"Mmmm," the boy said. He turned to his sister. "Would you pass it, please?" He pointed to a plate.

". . . not the bid," Marty said, "No. A *provision* . . ."

"Thank you," the boy said, and took the plate, and helped himself. His sister looked at him with large eyes. "Nobody knows what I'm thinking," she thought.

". . . and got the contract approved, and it's just a matter of the *endorsement* . . ."

"Uh huh," his wife said.

". . . of the *Overseers*."

"Overseers," she said, and nodded. "Beth, you want some more?" The little girl shook her head. "No, thank you," she said.

"*John?*"

"No, ma'am."

"And if I were dressed in brown velvet," she thought, "I could sit on a horse. But not a white horse.

Not at all. Or a black horse. But a Horse of Grey. A grey
horse with a black and brown mane," she thought. "And
I could braid it in patterns. What would I carry on
him?"

Later, down the street, at the school, she watched
her brother shooting baskets. She lay on the bleachers.
On her belly, The book and the school notebook open
on the bench before her, and her pencil crossways in her
mouth, like a bit.

And when they walked home she lagged behind, and
walked around the monument, till he turned back to
look for her.

The Green was deserted. On the far side, back at the
school, the last boys were leaving. Several cars slammed
their doors, as the parents started the drive home.

The clouds scudded in the moon, and the girl came
out from her walk around the monument, and came up
to him, and they walked down the street.

"Got your work done?" he said.

"Got it done," she said.

"Whatcha studying?"

"Stuff."

"Anything interesting?"

"Nope." They walked on.

"Miss Morressey treating ya . . . ?"

"She's okay."

"You like her?" She stopped and looked at him and
smiled.

"Nobody knows what I'm thinking," she thought,
"and the whole world was all watching *television*, and
we each had our own screen, n'everybody was watching

something *else,* but all we could see when we *looked* at them, was the back of the set, so all we knew, they were watching the same thing, n'that was all we know."

"What's sixteen times five?" he said. She looked at him gravely for a moment, then they both walked on.

"Clip clop, clip *clop,*" she thought. "Throughout the forest. Though you couldn't hear it, when they rode in the woods. Unless they were galloping fast. If he was a *messenger.* With special bags. Of bright black leather. 'Guard them with your life,' he said. And then he rode on."

He saw the food store was still open, and he took a pinch of loose material at the shoulder of her coat, and turned her toward the store.

Inside the store Carl stood at the register, paying for a six-pack of beer. The boy at the register looked up, and nodded to the boy and his sister.

"John," he said.

"James."

Carl took his change. "James, you tell your *father,* I'm going to come *lookin'* for him, at. that. time. *Bass* fishing," he said. "You tell him that now."

"I wn't have to tell him twice."

"Well, you tell him, how'vr many times it takes, cause I'm *coming* for him," he said, and left the store.

The girl took three long pretzel sticks from the container, and came up to the register.

". . . with his *sister,* and we thought that we . . ." her brother was saying. His friend widened his eyes, and John stopped speaking as his sister came up to the counter.

"One nickel," James said. She looked at her brother,

and he took the nickel from his jeans and put it on the platform of the small vegetable scale.

". . . one nickel," James said, absently, and flicked it across the scale, back toward John.

John looked down at it, then he flicked it back toward the other boy. It slid toward the edge of the scale, and stopped.

"How many downs?" James said.

"Three downs."

"Two downs," James said. "Two downs, you're such a fine, slick, *athlete* . . ."

"For?"

"A dollar."

"All right. So that's my first down," John said. He studied the nickel. It lay half an inch from the edge of the scale platform. He bent his face down close to it, and flicked the nickel very gently with the nail of his index finger. It slid to the edge of the scale, and lay, half on and half off the platform.

The girl, at the comic books, turned at the sound of the two boys shouting.

"Yes, Yes, Yes," John said. "*Yes!*"

"Ah, geddouddahere-you-pushed-it," the other boy said.

She looked at them jiving each other.

"No *wonder* that . . ." James said, and she turned back to look at the comics.

". . . and never grow up. For they found they *were* grown up." She thought. "Just like this picture. And the people loved to come to her, *miles around*. 'Oh, ask my Husband,' she would say. 'He is out riding.' "

She picked up a magazine, and turned to the back, where there were pictures of projects one could do at home. All of them dolls and gifts and coverings in calico and plaid, and simple directions on how to construct them. She flipped slowly through the pages.

"... and get *you* into a back room sometime, cause his sister *told* me!" James said, pointing at his friend, and grinning.

"You've spent so much time in this *store*," John said, and pointed back at the other boy.

"... *you* ..." James said, and leaned forward, jabbing his finger in the air, as if to wedge himself into the argument.

"... so much time *s'inn* here, in this *store,* that ..."

"You? You?" James said. "If you used one *tenth* the energy ..."

"... I"

"... wait a second. One *tenth,* against *Central,* that ..."

"Yes," she thought. "Yes."

The door opened, and a teenage couple, a boy and a girl, came in, and looked around, and moved between the two plywood racks of videos.

Beth replaced the magazine and walked to the counter.

"... n'stay *home* the rest of your life, n' ..."

"I ... I ..."

"Wait a second," James said, "and *meditate* on your sins: *Pride,* n' ..."

The girl put her hand under her brother's jacket, on the belt at the small of the back.

"*Okay.* Pick up your schoolbooks," he said. "Well. I'm going home."

His friend held out his palm, and John slapped it.

Leaving the store, Beth looked back, and saw the legs of the couple in the video racks. The boy put his face out, and looked shamefaced at her, and then he retreated.

They came out and started across the street. Beth looked back and saw the girl and boy, necking powerfully, behind the glass, behind the notices and flyers stuck in the inside of the store window.

"Sometime," she thought, "I will have something to sell. Or I will lose my dog. Or something. And I can put a card up there."

A car came down the street, traveling slowly. "Someone from town," John thought.

"Then I can put my own card up there," she thought. "That is how it works."

Henry looked out through the bedroom window.

"The fox came up through the trees," he said. He paused. "I saw it from the kitchen."

She looked at him and smiled to show that she knew he had said something pleasant.

"Would you . . ." he said, knowing the response.

"I loathe myself," he thought, as he continued. ". . . like to go for a walk?"

Her smile intensified. "Oh. Henry, that's a lovely idea," she said, "but . . ." She gestured to herself, clad in a nightgown.

He smiled, to indicate that he understood.

"Some other time," she said.

He nodded. "All right," he said.

"No," she said, "No. Don't be that way." She paused. "Please."

"What way is that?" he said.

"*Henry* . . ." she said. And sighed, and turned away, back to the mirror over her dresser.

He sat on the edge of the bed, and began removing his shoes.

"I was *late* today," he said, "behind a *man,* whose *truck went,* I think, about five miles an hour."

He took his low boots, and put them neatly underneath his bedside table.

"Uh huh," she said.

". . . and when I saw that he was not going to *stop* . . ." he said.

She left the room, and came back with a small white jar. She opened the jar, and began applying minute bits of cream to her face.

Henry walked to the window, and looked out at the lawn.

The moon had just risen, and the shadows were long. The lawn was striped light blue where the moon shone, and otherwise a black so soft as to be almost brown. "Well, if that ain't magic," he thought, "then I don't know what is."

" '. . . was going to stop' . . ." she said, and he turned.

"What?" he said.

"The man was never going to stop."

"What man?"

"What man? The truckdriver."

His mind raced. ". . . the truckdriver . . . ?" he said.

She turned to him. She had the white jar in her left hand, and a small dollop of cream on the upturned first fingers of her right.

". . . the truckdriver," he thought. "The truckdriver who was never going to stop. Who could that be? Except the man on the road today. How could she know of that?" he thought. And then he rememered he'd told her, and wondered why he had; and he felt shame, beyond which was the feeling that he had confessed, and had not been forced to, and it was his own doing.

"I saw him on the road," he said. "And he was *driving*; we were on 18, and he was *before* me.

"Mile after mile," he said, his voice sounding hollow to him; then he was out of it, and he felt that the story continued of its own, empty and horrible, as she turned back to the mirror. And he hardly heard his voice, as he turned to the window, and looked out at the lawn. In the West there was still the briefest band of bright blue above the trees.

"The animals will be down on the pond soon," he thought. "Down on the pond, and a man who was sufficiently quiet could be *down* there. . . :" He breathed in the night air. It was full and thrilling, as it only was at the end of the Summer, when it started to get cold at night, and it was wild and comforting at the same time.

Once he'd seen bear on the pond. A sow and two cubs. Looking, at the first, like dogs. "Like black dogs," he thought. "And there is the panther out there."

Lynn said he had seen that, too; once, at dusk, down the road. When he was a boy.

"...and every time I'd pull out to pass," he said, "...not that there are all that many *places* . . ."

"...there's that one," she said.

"Down at the hill, yes," he heard himself say. "But wouldn't you know it . . ."

"um hmmmmmm . . ." she said.

"...as soon as I got far enough over to see *past* him . . . :" She nodded.

"...there's another car coming down . . ." She flicked off the light and came back to the bed. She walked around to her side, and stood by her bedside table. She began removing her watch and earrings.

"...and that's about *it*," he said. He stood between the window and the bed. She looked around and smiled at him.

"Oh, yes," he thought. " 'That's right,' she's saying. 'See how easy it is?' "

He smiled back.

"Now, what would I do now?" he thought. "I'd stand here and sigh. Or yawn. I'd yawn and say something, and go to the bathroom."

"Waaalll . . ." he said, and yawned. He found the yawn came naturally, and was surprised and grateful it did.

"Waall, I guess . . ." he said, and yawned again. She nodded. She stepped out of her slippers and into the bed.

He walked to the bathroom. As he did he heard her

bedside light click off, and the room was immediately striped in blue shadows.

The mullions threw a tilted lattice over the floor and up the wall and the door to the hall. He opened it, breaking the pattern, and found himself in the hall. He closed the door softly behind him.

Down the stair the living room was washed in the blue light, and the house was cool and almost cold. He walked halfway down the staircase and sat.

He heard her moving, heavily, interrogatorily, and for his benefit, in the bed.

She rearranged herself. "Where are you, and what are you doing?" the sounds meant. "What are you doing?"

"No," he thought. "No. I can sit here for one moment now."

Rose drove down the morning street. Over the bridge she saw the sedan with out-of-state plates parked, the engine running. She knew this girl was in there with some man. "One day," she thought, "they're going to find her dead in the woods."

She saw James, as he turned on the lights in the food store. She turned the radio off, and the lights, as she pulled her car up outside the Post Office. She sighed and she fumbled in her pockets for the keys.

Five

The excellent relief of the fan lulled him. He sat at the counter in the empty store. He'd dusted and cleaned the store, and come back to the utility sink to scrub his hands and remove the smell of the cleansers.

He sat, his foot up in a high rung of the stool, the stool leaning back, wedged into the small cash register alcove. . . . The day was hot. He'd taken the fan from its protective plastic bag, back in the storage area, and set it up on the counter.

He was of two minds about the plastic bag. Each time he took the fan out he appreciated the absence of dust; but he also husbanded a small feeling — almost a guilt — against himself for his concision in the treatment of a machine that was, after all, a luxury; perhaps, he thought, just the weak luxury of a weak man.

"But it's my store," he thought, "and if they want to berate me, well, they can shop somewhere else." He clucked his tongue, as if to say ". . . and that's that."

"And who is there doesn't enjoy comfort?" he

thought, surveying, in his mind, the townspeople, and their various, and, he'd allow, legitimate concessions to the human need for comfort.

His hands smelled of soap, and the floor cleanser. Each time the fan came around it fluttered the receipt pad on the counter, and raised the smell on his hands. "... everyone ..." he thought, and his eyes began to close. "Just a minute," he thought, "hot day." The fan, as he listened to it, sounded like a breath. "Like a woman's breath," he thought. "Coming around," he thought. "Coming around. First time you hear it. Swiveling. And the soft hum of the blades. Whoever designed it did it well. Like someone in bed next to you. Sleeping," he thought. "Lovely, fine invention. Moving the air."

His shadow relaxed, and his head started to come forward on his chest. "Bert Wheeler's got an air conditioner," he thought, "but his wife don't seem to ..."

Twaing. He came awake, hearing the *twaing twaing* as a car drove over the hose, out by the gas pumps. He blinked and said, "Huh."

He brought the stool down and looked around the empty store.

Out at the gas pumps was a low, white convertible, its top down. A man and a woman sat in the car. Dick sighed and rubbed his face and got down from the stool. He walked the few steps to the front door, surveying the store. "... *all right,*" he thought; as if the store had made a request, and he were responding. "All right."

He let the screen door slam behind him, and walked out to the pumps, squinting his eyes against the sun. He got the nozzle, and screwed open the car's gas cap. The driver got out of the car, stretching himself, as after a long drive.

"Fill it?" Dick said. The man nodded. He was athletically built, in his mid-thirties; and he wore tight blue jeans and a grey t-shirt. He put his hands flat on the side of the car and pushed his legs back, one after the other, stretching out his calves, revealing two-tone cowboy boots, brown on the bottom, and cream colored above. He stood, and rolled his head around to his shoulder.

"Long drive?" Dick said. There was a moment's lag, as if the man were far enough away for the sound to require a while to reach him; then he turned to Dick and smiled, and shook his head. His smile saying, "Yes, I understand that you're being sociable."

Dick drew his breath in slightly. He walked to the far side of the gas island. As he did, he saw the man glance at the woman, his mouth slightly open, as if commenting on Dick — as if there had been something droll in his behavior.

Dick bent to pick the squeegee out of the water bucket. He wicked the excess water off, and walked to the passenger side to clean the car's window.

"Now, I do not want to look at that girl," he thought; "I'm not coming here to look at her, and damn him if he thinks so. Not that I give a fuck what he thinks, but you tell me, how am I going to clean the windshield, without picking up the windshield wiper?"

He bent over the hood, and picked the windshield wiper up, and turned to clean the window. As he did he found the woman looking at him.

He saw her face, completely composed, and looking

at him as if it were the most natural thing in the world for them to be facing each other, inches apart, through the piece of glass. She was perfectly beautiful. A woman in her late twenties, with dark brown hair cut short, an olive complexion, and her cheeks burnt by the sun.

Her large eyes looked at him, and he was stunned by his inability to categorize her look.

". . . am I . . . ? Am I . . . ? Am I . . . ?" he thought. "She is not inviting, or questioning, or angry, or . . ." he thought.

She looked at him. And he realized that he had become immobile, and should continue cleaning the windshield. But the woman did not seem embarrassed.

"I know that she must be mocking me," he thought. "Why doesn't she look like it? What does she mean?" He thought of various excuses for staying on her side of the car; then he simply looked away from her.

The man was standing by the driver's door, faced in the woman's direction. As Dick came around to the driver's side, he saw the woman look at the man, and the man's eyes widen and twinkle slightly. Dick stole a glance at her, through the windshield, and she felt his gaze and looked up; this time, he thought, with a polite but definite interrogation, as if saying, ". . . yes . . . ?" He looked away.

He heard the *clunk* as the gas pump shut off. He moved awkwardly past the man, back to the island. He dropped the squeegee back into the pail. He glanced at the pump, although he had seen the total earlier. "Fourteen *eleven*," he said, smiling at the man.

He fitted the nozzle back into the pump, and screwed the gas cap back on.

Then he straightened up and took a handkerchief from his back pocket. He wiped his hands, and sniffed once, as he walked behind the car and over to the driver, who had taken out his wallet.

The man handed Dick a ten and a five. Dick, nodding, took them. "... *yessir,*" he said. He cursed himself for a clown, as he dug in his pocket for the change.

"Lord, let me have the right change," he thought. "Do not let me have to say, 'Be right back,' go to get change, and have him say, 'Forget about it,' or ..." He brought his hand out of his pocket, and counted out the change.

"Eleven, and *four,*" he said, "and a dime for twenty-five, and senny-five makes fifteen." He dropped the change in the driver's hand.

"And I'm *not* gonna say, 'You all come back,' or 'Have a nice day,' or any of that country trash. And these people can rot in hell," he thought, "the two of them," as the man slung himself into the driver's seat and started up the car. He glanced in the rearview mirror and reached up his right hand to adjust it.

As he did, the woman turned back and looked at Dick. The car drove off and Dick stood there; in the street, watching them drive off — watching the woman turn back away from him, and shake her hair out once, as the car dipped and disappeared down the hill.

Lynn heard the jay first. It was over the rise and down in the draw below, so it was not his dog and him that the jay was scolding.

The dog stopped and cocked his head. Lynn patted his thigh twice, and the dog came over to him.

Lynn pointed a finger at him, and the dog sat. He passed his hand, parallel, flat to the ground, and the dog lay down.

The jay continued scolding as Lynn came up over the ridge. Across the draw, at the edge of a logging road, the sun was glinting off the windshield trim of a truck. Lynn came back down, and circled to his right. He rounded the edge of the ridge, and saw, down in a bend of the bank of the dry stream, Maris and the man making love.

He watched them for a moment, then retraced his steps.

Back at the bottom of the rise, the dog picked up her head at Lynn's approach. He tapped his hands on the front of his thighs, and the dog bounded up to him and came to heel.

Lynn, unconsciously, turned back on the usual path of their walk. As he started forward, the dog went on ahead, jumping and nosing in the leaves.

He realized the usual walk would take them over the ridge, and upon the couple down below, so he clucked to the dog. As she turned around, Lynn made a sweeping gesture to his left, and started walking out that way. The dog straightened her neck, to question him, and Lynn repeated the gesture.

The dog trotted parallel to Lynn, some twenty yards to his right, along the ridge bottom. They headed back past Lynn's cabin, and over the field on the far side.

They walked through an overgrown apple orchard. Lynn walked past a twisted, grey trunk, and broke a scale off the bark and put it between his front teeth and worked it back and forth.

The dog ran through the cover up ahead; and, every twenty seconds or so, glanced back at the man, who nodded, absently, "... that's all right. Go on. I'm pleased with you."

The dog nosed the leaves at the bottom of the old orchard. "Yep. I know. They're in there," Lynn thought. "Don't you worry. We'll gettem ..."

The birds liked the apple orchard, and its proximity to the road, and the road salt. Lynn saw them, all year long, along and in the road. "The Brazen Partridge," Lynn thought — except in the Season, and they went to ground, and you couldn't see them without the dog. "If that ain't thinking, what is?" Lynn said softly.

They came out, through the orchard, on the hill above the road, and walked down in the sunlight. The dog stopped at the road and waited.

"All right," Lynn said to himself, "Good. All right. I got lucky in you."

He came down to the road. He took the old web lead from the pocket of his chore coat, and *thwacked* it against his leg, as he came out into the road, and the dog came to heel.

They walked in the afternoon sun, two miles down the road, descending all the while. Off to the left ranks of mountains, hill after hill, receded till the last rank mixed with the clouds, and one could not tell at once if it was a mountain or a cloud.

They walked down the road as it closed in, and then they were between two overhanging banks of trees. The road closed over and behind them as they wound down the long hill. The dog was showing off, proud to stay at the man's heel, though he knew she suspected that he'd simply forgotten to free her from the command.

And, at the bottom of the long hill, another dirt road intersected them, and they turned right. "*Okay. G'wan!*" Lynn said, and the dog looked at him, then shot forward up the road, getting home.

Lynn breathed a bit heavily as he climbed again. He heard the engine as it topped the hill, and the truck came over the crest and down toward him, moving too fast.

It was the same truck he'd seen on the logging road. The driver was alone in the cab; and Lynn got a glimpse of him, scowling, and pointedly not noticing the pedestrian, as he flew past.

Lynn stepped off the road. The truck's rear wheels scattered pebbles and stones. It came down to the intersection, turned wide to the right as the driver changed gears, and started down the road to town. Lynn turned back from watching it, and walked up this hill.

He reached the crest. Below he saw the dog, turning into the small trail that led to his cabin; and, beyond that, just coming over the next hill, Maris, on her walk back to town.

When he took the level to it, then it worked.

There was a thing called adjusting the beat, or regulating the beat, or some such thing, that he had heard, which meant listening to determine that the interval between the one beat and the next was even.

"You don't want," Charlie had told him, "you don't want it to be '*tick*-tock,' do you see? Or the opposite; but 'tock-tock-tock . . .' and so on. N'that *bad* sound," Charlie had said, "is cause, the clock's not sitting level." What Charlie had not told him was this: If the beat was not regular, the clock would not run.

As to the chimes, he'd heard it when he'd first received it, as a present. He'd heard it out in the garden, chiming, and thought, "I've never heard the Church clock up here before." He'd gone on raking, before he thought, "It must be an aberration in the *weather*. I know that on a fine day, in high pressure, both sights and sounds from far off appear closer."

He'd gone on raking, and then thought, "But it is not, I don't think, a particularly fine day. Not so I'd remark it."

And then he thought he was three miles up from the Village, and remembered he'd never heard the Church clock chime, and wondered if it had a chime at all. It could not be the chiming of a clock down in the Village, or in any further village that existed thereabout, or bells, or anything, he thought, but the clock on the mantel — the sound altered — "By what?" he wondered.

"Well, the wind, the reflection of sound by some condition in the atmosphere, maybe the condition of the case of the clock itself, if it had been altered by the day, by heat, or by *humidity* . . ."

The case of the clock was black metal. It bore small, golden stencils of wheat. The clock stood, three-quarters of a foot high, on the mantel, on the brick, in back of the woodstove. And many times he'd lie in bed at night, listening to it comfort him.

When it first stopped he'd tried to fix it himself, his knowledge of a technique to aid him limited to checking to see if it was wound — it was; or if overwound — which, as far as he could tell, it was not. He'd opened the back to make sure that the pendulum swung free, which it did.

Later he'd taken it to a man in Town who'd charged him ten dollars and told him the clock ran perfectly well. But Henry, when he took it home, could never get it to run again.

He subconsciously attributed its stoppage to some lack in himself — to some flaw. "Else, why would it stop?" he thought.

Through several years the clock sat there, stopped at something after three. And his wife dusted it, and did not seem discontent that it did not run.

When he looked at it, he did so with a low-level remorse, and with resignation, as if to say, "I'm the kind of man — as I know — who lives on that sort of level, and I suppose that there's nothing wrong with that."

"The sound of a Village Clock. In some Victorian Novel," he thought. "People lived simpler then. How could they not? Of course they had some foibles. But they were not assaulted constantly. Assaulted."

"The sound of a Village Clock." He tried to describe it to several people, and had. The first time he heard it, even taken his wife out in the back, by the garden, to hear it. He'd waited till just before it was to chime, and he went to get her, allowing that amount of time he knew that he'd require to explain, at greater length, he knew, than possibly could be required for simple transmissions of intelligence, as she pretended, for reasons he almost understood, and did not want to understand, a lack of comprehension.

He allowed an amount of time for her to be persuaded to come outside. But, when she came, it did not sound like the village clock, not like the perfect village clock in a novel, and not like a village clock at all.

And he had to allow her — even discounting this second instance as a mere regression-to-the-norm (for how could this second instance be as startling, and, so, as beautiful as the first?) — even allowing for that natural erosion, it did not, he admitted to himself, and, in a lesser way, to her, sound like a Church bell, like a Village Clock at all.

He could not feel rancor. She was right. Something *material,* as he put it to himself, something physical and real had changed. That freak concatenation of circumstance that pitched the sound was not repeated. Neither with his wife, or otherwise. Never again, not even vaguely, did the clock exhibit what he had come to think of as "that trick."

And then it had stopped running altogether.

And, now and again, he would look at it, stopped. "Some things," he'd think, and he would not finish his thought.

But one day — "Isn't that always the way that it is?" he thought, thinking back on it — he straightened from feeding the stove, and there was the clock, and he looked at it. He looked at it a long while.

Without framing the thought consciously, he walked back into the mudroom and took the small level from the toolbox and took it back to the clock.

"It *looks* level," he thought, "but in an old house, as we know, you have to do it by eye. Everything so out-of-plumb — you *fix* it, you have to do it by *eye*. You do it to the *level* . . ." he thought, excusing himself to some unknown antagonist, "it will look *skewed*. So it is not *unlikely* the mantel's out-of-plumb.

"But even if it is," he thought, "does the clock not belong — of course it does, it's proved it — in that category of things which do not work, and which defy all effort and science in the attempt to retrieve them?

"Some things are like that," he thought. "If they were not, how would we live our lives? We are not *God* . . ."

But another voice spoke, and it said, "There is that category of things which are susceptible to the application of First Principles." And he put the small level on the clock, on the top of its case, flush with the front. It showed out-of-plumb to a degree greater than he would have thought possible, and he was elated.

He went to the kindling box, and snapped a chip of wood and came back and shimmed it under the low end of the clock, thinking he would surely overbalance it in the other direction. But the level said not, the chip was insufficient, and the clock still canted; and he took another chip and shoved it underneath the first. He jimmied it in and out, until he got the bubble centered, and the clock rested perfectly true.

He looked at it as at a wonder.

He reached to the top of the case, behind, careful not to disturb the level, and found the key.

He swung open the glass cover on the dial, and tried the tension of the two springs, the main drive, and that which fed the chimes, inserting the key in first one, and then in the other winding aperture; he found both springs fully wound.

He closed the cover and replaced the key on top of the case. He reached delicately behind to the clock's back, and pivoted up the door to the works. His fingers found the pendulum, and pushed it, ever so lightly, to get it swinging. He let the door to the works swing down, and stepped back, listening to the sound of the clock.

He stood, listening to the ticking of the clock.

"Well, yes, is it going to stop? Sometimes," he thought, "like a watch, that's laid for twenty-five years in a drawer. You pick it up, and the action of the jar to the mechanism, will cause it to *run,* for ten, f'teen seconds . . ." But the clock kept ticking. And when he was satisfied that it would run, he took it down and placed it on the table. He checked the time against his watch, and started to set the clock.

"Slowly," he thought. "*Slowly.* For you do not want to wreck it now. And there's no reason not to take All the Time in The World."

He opened the glass cover and moved the minute hand through the half-hour. It chimed once. He waited a moment, and moved it through the hour, and waited while it chimed seven times, and then waited another moment to make sure that the mechanism had come to rest.

He was relieved that the number of chimes matched the time on the face, and would have thought it harsh if he'd gotten it running, only to find it crippled in some serious way, in some way beyond both his knowledge and intuition.

He continued turning the clock through the hours, delighted to hear its chimes again. He turned it through the last half-hour especially slowly, with a gravity he excused to himself as simple, mechanical wisdom. "I wouldn't want to ruin it now, through *haste*," he thought. "Wouldn't that be ironic? Wouldn't that be just like me?"

When he'd set the time, he checked the clock against his watch again, and brought it back to the mantel and rested it, once more, on the wood chips.

He leveled it again, and was about to jog the pendulum, when he thought better of it, and advanced the minute hand one minute to allow for the time he'd spent at the mantel. He closed the glass cover, and reached behind and jogged the pendulum, and once again, the clock began to run.

There was the level. He was looking at the level. What more could he do? Why had he not taken the level down? "*Because,*" he thought, "because there are *two planes,*" he thought, pleased with himself, and pleased to feel entitled to his pleasure. "Two planes in which it rests, in each of which it could need adjustment."

He stepped up and, gingerly, pivoted the level ninety degrees, so that it sat across the top of the clock, front-to-back. He leaned around to see the bubble, and was disappointed to find that the clock was level in this plane as well.

"Well," he thought, and sighed. He took the level down, and stood there, listening. "And soon it will strike those three times," he said to himself.

He sat on the couch, an echo in the back of his mind repeating, "Yes. It will."

"It will chime once at twelve-thirty; again, once at one; and again once at one-thirty."

He tried to think if there were a fourth time, or if there were another series, at some other time, in which the clock would behave in such a way. He found, as he found every time he asked himself the question, that there was not, and was disappointed for a moment.

"Why should I be disappointed?" he thought. "What do I care?" He shook his head. "That's a perfect example."

There was a great comfort in being part of a group; and it was, he thought, similar to the comfort of being alone. If you took the trappings off, he thought, it felt the same; and much of it was just the lack of need for speech.

The Trooper sat in a small, flat-bottomed skiff on the lake. It had been twilight for what seemed like hours, and looked to continue so for some hours more. It was cold and felt like rain coming on; but it wasn't humid, he thought, just a touch of chill.

Off in the reeds a marsh harrier glided, looking for prey.

"What keeps 'em up?" he thought, as it continued, wings still, long past the time when he would have thought it would have to land, or beat the air for altitude. He watched it glide, its path straight as a razor cut, skimming the tops of the reeds, until the time his mind, satisfied that it could glide forever, ceased to wonder at the flight; then the bird beat its wings once, and climbed, and veered into the woods.

"And I can tell her later," he thought, "how lovely the hawk was." He reeled in the last of his line, and made another cast in the reeds, and began taking it in.

"Something more than slowly," he thought, "that's right."

He was alone on the lake. The few scattered camps were empty. From the shore, someone looking on would have seen a man in a black slicker and a floppy green cap, sitting low in the boat which drifted slowly inland with the wind.

He reeled in and unsnapped the small gold spinner from the leader. He opened his tackle box and looked at the contents a moment. He dropped the spinner in a compartment, and took a red and white striped spoon, snapped it on the line, closed the case, and put it back beneath his seat. He made a cast toward the reeds, and began to reel it in.

"And she might say, 'Well, certainly 'm,' she might say; 'it's so beautiful, why don't you take me, *too*?' " he thought.

"Or perhaps not say it, but think it. Which would be like her. To *think* it, but not express it, because it speaks for itself.

"But she's not a bad girl, by any stretch of the imagination," he thought; "and why should I tax her with things she can't understand and which would seem discourtesy. And maybe she's *right*," he thought, "and I should just keep the hawk to myself; *and* the loons, *and* the blue heron; or damn well *ask* her to come out with me."

He reached between his feet, and loosened a beer from the plastic holder. He popped it open, and took a small sip, and put the can down carefully between his feet. He reeled in the line, and put the pole in the boat, leaning it against the seat opposite him. He put out the oars, and began to row away from the weeds.

"I," he thought, "I don't want sympathy, understanding, or a special break from anyone that lives." He put his back into it, and rowed out from the small bay into the body of the lake. The rowing warmed him and made his back feel strong, as if his shoulder muscles extended from his neck to his waist. "*Rowing*," he thought and breathed deep.

He watched the drops from the oars drip on the lake's surface, as he brought them up for another stroke. The boat moved past the point, and out into the lake. He put the oars up on the gunwales, picked up his rod, and stood.

The boat still glided forward. He made a cast over the stern. The lure flew some fifty yards, and fell. He turned the handle, and the bail on the reel clicked over and he started taking in line.

The fish hit, and he was shocked. It bent the rod over, and his heart stopped. "Oh, shit," he thought;

"don't let me lose it." He started reeling in, keeping the tip of his rod high as he could, to keep the hook set.

"The net. Now where's the net . . . ?" He looked down at his feet. He saw the net in the bow of the boat, five feet off. He sat and crabbed himself over the two seats, toward the bow, keeping the line taut, and taking slack when the fish gave him any.

" 'Fish for dinner,' and I'm not going to think it," he thought. He reached down with one hand, to grab the net, pulling back on the rod to keep the tension up. The fish broke the surface twelve feet away, the mouth and head pink and red and green. "Oh, hell," he thought, "it is a monster."

He put both hands on the rod, and tilted it up, and took in line.

"You think I wanted you *before* . . . ?" he thought. "I want you *now*."

It broke the surface again, trying to spit out the hook. "In *Hell*," he thought; "the longest day that you were born."

He knelt and stole a moment to take the left oar, and move the boat, so to put the bass along its side. The fish was four feet off. He left the oar in the water, and wrenched the rod up once again, and took in the slack. He looked down at the thrashing fish. "It's like the first time you're going to get laid," he thought, "and you cannot believe it, but you know it's going to be." He tugged the rod back over the boat, pulling the fish closer. There it was.

"You son of a *bitch*," he thought.

"You son of a bitch. Get your ass in here." He

tugged the fish closer. "*Oh* yes," he thought. "Gentle, my ass." It thrashed its tail up. He saw the bright white on its underbelly. "That's right," he thought. "One mother-fucking second." His left hand reached for the handle of the net, on the seat; but his motion dislodged it, and it fell into the bottom of the boat.

The fish was alongside. He suppressed an impulse to reach in and grab it with his hand. He leaned forward, keeping his eyes on the fish, and feeling for the net in the bottom of the boat.

He took his eye from the fish and dared a glance for the net. He saw it, and his hand found it, and he came around to net the fish, as the line went slack.

"All right," he thought, "but *that's* not what that means."

He raised the rod, as if, in one chance in ten thousand, the fish had somehow, and contrary to all experience, gotten line and dived; as if he'd find it there, still on the end of his line, still fighting, still there, just trying a different tactic.

"And that can happen," he thought; as he sat, shamed and empty, and with the feeling of a loss, and no one to blame but himself.

"I fought it too hard, or I didn't tie the *leader* right, or . . ." he thought, as he reeled in the line, to the naked end.

He sat in the boat, in a pose that might have looked like a man thinking. But he wasn't thinking. A wind blew up and the boat started to twist in the water. He looked down, questioningly, and saw the oar, still in the water, and put it inside the boat.

Down the lake two blue herons were flying, just above the trees, impossibly huge, long legs behind them. He watched for a moment, before they dipped down. In the dusk, he couldn't see if they'd gone behind or down in front of the trees. The shadows merged, and they were gone.

He squinted up his eyes. He slowly turned in his seat, and looked at the lake. A wind blew ripples in a line two hundred yards from him. He felt small drops of rain on the back of his hands, and looked down to see rain peppering the water. He watched the rain for a moment. He smiled and bent over to open his tackle box.

"It was hot," he thought. "It was so hot that, as the Bible had it, 'the sky was iron and the earth was brass.' "

It was so hot it could not be taken other than as a punishment. The two kestrel chicks were in the road, just as he'd heard they were. Down at the Store they all were talking about it; and how, one-by-one, they each had stopped and shooed them back, into the woods. How the chicks had gone reluctantly, back off the road and into the scrub.

"What are they in the road for?" Henry had asked, and they told him salt, left from the Winter; and grit, to put in their craw — though no one knew for certain if that was the case.

One said, "I know it's true of partridge," and they had tried to pair the features of partridges and chickens as they understood them — for they all were certain that both needed grit, down in their gullet, to digest their food.

So they compared the acknowledged habits of that group to those of the hawk, and, so, guessed if the hawk was like them in that one respect.

Salt, and grit, they said, and no one could think of a third reason for them to be in the road.

But now Henry could.

For on the way down to town he'd seen them, just below the Rise, just as the other men at the store had described them, like some landmark, retailed from one navigator to another. And he'd left the car and shooed them back out of the road.

Now, coming back from town, there was the one of them, perched on his dead sibling. And Henry got down and looked at it — . The rich tawny-red back, and the brown-and-white wings and the vast liquid black eyes of the hawk chick looked up at him, as he thought, pleadingly. He went to the side of the road to find a stick to scrape the dead bird into the woods.

"I wouldn't want the one flying up in my face, with that beak, with those claws, and clawing me," he thought.

"If he is going to stay there, on his lost Mate, let me get it off the road, and into the woods." He searched for a good stout stick. "What is it," he thought, "that impels them? Some instinct of mutual aid? But what could it serve? And it's not its Mate. It's its brother or sister. Still, it's instructive, that it is staying there," he thought, as he came back to the birds, where the one was eating the corpse of the other.

And Henry thought, and smiled like a miser, "I know the third reason the birds were in the road. The men at the Store never thought of: to peck at some dead animal that had been killed there. A squirrel, or a chipmunk, or a mouse, or a toad, ground into the road, and they were eating it."

The kestrel chick put one black eye on him, as he stood, holding the stick. "This would look incriminating," he thought, "given the facts, but if one didn't know know the history. One could interpret my holding the stick as aggressive to the bird; as if I were angry that I had killed the other; or as if I wanted to fight it, for its kill. Though, perhaps, that is ludicrous," he thought, "a man as big as me, fighting that little bird. And I'm not saying," he thought, "that I know its nature — just that I am marginally less deluded than the men in the Store."

Dick sat at his desk upstairs. The column-lined ledger lay open before him, and he looked at it with his jaw set.

In the far room the noise of his wife putting up the dishes grated on him, and he looked toward the half-open study door.

"And she will come *in* here and *say* something," he thought, "and I'll tell her, 'For chrissake, I am trying to *work*; and what do you *expect* from a man? To be a God?, and kiss the ass of those shitheads, ten hours a day every day, and then come up here, and have to deal with your requests while I have to pore over our receipts looking for figures that just aren't there, and . . .' " He stopped, as the soft clatter in the kitchen stopped.

"Fine," he thought, "and now I'm sposed to wonder what you're doing, and when you'll be in." He said,

"*Huh.*" He listened to the kitchen sounds, but could neither hear nor sense his wife in there.

"Well, all right, then," he thought; "and what a swine I am. To want to take it out on her. She works like a dog; and I don't know a thing about her, finally, except she works as hard as I do, and she has the kids, and all I do is bitch about it, and I should get down on my knees and pray her forgiveness for my sins."

He looked down at the figures on the page. "Hell of a world," he thought. "Hell of a goddamned world. N'here I'm an old fart."

Three sharpened pencils lay on the desk, across the top of the ledger. He put the pencil in his hand down on the desk, and took one of the new ones up.... He erased an entry on the page, and brushed the gum off with the side of his hand.

He turned the ledger back several pages, ran his fingers down a column, until he came to the entry he wished, then he nodded, and lifted his hand, as if to say, "*There* it is. I told you that *that* was the culprit; and, now, you see, it works *out.*"

"Sir," he thought, "this is a *business . . .*"

"Here is the problem. Do you see?" And pointed at the entry on the sheet, ". . . and don't you tell me otherwise. God *Damn* it, man, unless you've sat behind that counter twelve hours a day for the last fifteen years . . .

"You see that figure? You see that dot? It's a decimal point. That little dot there, and the figure to the right of it is an eight. And then a one. Eighty-one cents. Eighty-one cents an hour, which is what, after fifteen years, my wife and I make si'in in that store, running that store.

"Eighty-one cents an hour, while you have the gall, you vicious swine, to say that I have cheated the bank.

"Eighty-one cents an hour, which is the price of not going along. *You* go along. You've got a nice job. You've got a paycheck, and you've prolly got a contract, and your life is set and booming; and I went out and I bought this store."

He heard a plate clink in the kitchen and turned to see a glimpse of his wife.

"Cheated the bank," he said to himself.

"Eighty-one cents an hour; and if I were a better man I could include my wife slaving like a saint, which she does, and all the sacrifices she has made, but I'm not fit to say it. I treat her like shit. A better man would say, 'And how do you think it makes a man feel to see his wife, who expected great things from him, and threw her lot in with him, year after year, for *nothing*; and no *money*, and no *equity*, and not *complaining*, and going along with this shit-poor program her man got her in? And how do you think that that makes me feel?'

"But I'm not even fit to say that," he thought; "and it would be trammeling my legitimate feelings for her to *presume* to trade upon her sacrifices and tell that cocksucker how I feel. And if I were a better man . . ." he thought.

His wife came in the room holding a small jelly jar with liquor in it, and put it on a corner of his desk, and went and sat down on the couch.

". . . and here she's done that, and I spend all day eyeing the young girls who come in, and here she's just done that, and what the hell kind of a piece of shit am I, I swear to God. I swear to my Creator."

And he turned around and felt that he was glaring at her, as she sat on the couch.

"What?" he said.

"Kids asleep."

"Uh huh," he said.

She took a cigarette pack from the pocket of her cardigan, and drew her feet beneath her on the couch. She lit a cigarette, and blew the smoke out. "Drink your drink," she said.

"Was good of you to bring it to me," he said. She looked at him and smiled.

"Down the Post Office they said Lou Miller beat up on Sally Foster again," she said.

"She tell the Police?"

"Nope," she said, shrugging one shoulder to say, "as we would expect." "I *think* she's going to kill him one day."

"Well, I wish she would," he said.

". . . and we did not get the right count on those four-fourteens from Binghamton."

". . . you're shitting me . . ." he said.

". . . because . . . I wisht that I *was*," she said.

"You're sure?"

"I am," she said.

"We send 'em back?"

"I packed 'em, n'they're waitin' on U.P.S. tomorrow," she said. He shook his head.

". . . *innit?*" she said. He took a drink, and she said, this time to herself, ". . . innit . . ."

"N'that's fine for *her*," he thought. "That's her *nature*. Goddammit to hell, but that's the truth. Things don't get to her like they do to me, and she has that ability to just live through it."

"I talked to the bank," he said, "and, the midst, the same old shit, the *loan,* and . . ."

"Uh huh . . ." she said.

". . . he starts *in* . . ." he said, and blew his breath out through clenched teeth, "he starts in . . ."

She got up from the couch and came over to the chair beside his desk and sat there listening to him. "Well," she thought, "he is putting on some weight; but not as much as some do, in their forties. That's the time."

". . . how I am *cheating* him . . ." he said. She made a small sound and shook her head sadly. Dick went on speaking. She picked up the jelly jar, and took a sip of whiskey. "That's the time," she thought. "And how the hell can it be easy, sitting in that store all the time; sitting in that store. And I'm not that big a help, either," she thought.

"*Isn't* it?" she said. "*Isn't* it . . . ?"

"It is," she said.

"You know it is," he said, "because I've got it right here." He picked the ledger up with both hands, then lowered it back to the desk. "I want to tell you something," he said. She edged her chair in closer, as he prepared to speak.

". . . course, he is a *big* son of a bitch," she thought. "And, attractive, as they are, those rough ones, at some point they always choose to start beatin' up on *you.*" Dick paused, and his wife nodded, in response to his request for agreement.

"Sally Foster, or no one's the least bit different; cause they're like wild animals," she thought.

"... F'they're crazy, they'll tell you right off; N'if you *go* with them, well, then, you've been warned. N'here is *this* guy, beats his wife, I hope to tell you, and the stuff we never hear of, much *too* much as we might just imagine it. And I hope the Troopers gettem, and knock him around a bit, because it's a crime and a sin against God, beat up on a woman like he did to her. Well, 'n I should thank God for my Blessings."

Dick took a sip of whiskey and glanced at the desk. She put the cigarette pack next to the ledger, and he took one and lit it as he spoke.

"Thank you," he said.

"I'm sorry, hon," she said.

"Well, *hell*," he said. They sat in silence together.

"... but those slim hips," she thought. "So cocky, comes in here those tight jeans ..."

"... *huh*" Dick said.

"... you could see why they fall for her," she thought. "That's the God's Truth."

"N'you wrapped the four-fourteens with the invoice, senn 'em back to Binghamton ... ?" he said.

"I did," she said.

"I know you did," he thought. "Because you always get it right. I bitch and moan like a woman, but *you* are the one. I'm falling apart, you keep it moving. See:" he thought, "this is a different view of life. As if you've been *raised* differently, or something," he thought. "Something *basic*.

"... and I'll do the other invoices in the morning," she said.

"Well don't worry about it," he said. "Fucken store's gone be *gone*, this time next week, some *other* sucker have it." She smiled at him. "I mean it," he said. "How much c'n a man take?" She rose and kissed him on the crown of his head, and she hugged his head to her stomach. He pressed his head toward her.

She looked around the room. There were old sporting goods calendars on the walls, the framed twenty-dollar bill, a photo of the store as it had been in 1895. "Well, there's no gas pumps," she thought. "Apart from that, it's about the same. The life's probably the same, too. Same hours."

He sighed.

"... merchandise probably a damn sight better then," she thought. "Apart from that ..."

"Well, she had *diabetes*, or something," he said. "I don't know what it is ..."

"How do you know she had it?" she said.

"Cause the way she smelled." He levered himself back up the bed, so his back was flat against the headboard. He took a deep breath.

"Like *chocolate*," he said. "It smells like *chocolate*, and as if someone's haddin wiped their ass. I think that that is diabetes."

"Is it tough to touch them?" she said.

She was sitting on the chair by the dressing table, by

the window. She had on a white t-shirt, and nothing else. He looked at her.

"We had a fella . . ." he said, and he stopped.

"What . . . ?"

"We had a fella . . ." he said, and he thought back to the corpse blown back on the floor, the chair on its side; the automatic, hammer back, lying where the man's dead hand had dropped it.

". . . and I was surprised it didn't *discharge* again, when it hit the floor."

"What?" she said; and he looked at her and realized he had been speaking.

"Fella shot himself," he said. "And there he's sitting with his girlfriend, both of 'em drunk. He's cleaning his gun, it seems. Jim, the barracks, says they were having a *squabble,* as he sees it. And he's at the table, cleaning his pistol; and he claps it together, and he says something to her like '*Someday* . . .' "

The girl in the t-shirt nodded.

" 'Someday'. . ." And he mimed a man putting a gun to his head.

"And '*Blang!*' "

"*Huh,*" she said.

"And that's *his* story," he said.

"And you put the gloves on for *him,*" she said.

"Yes. I did," he said.

On the call the woman had been shrieking, running down the road with a man's flannel shirt misbuttoned, out, over her jeans. In house slippers, running in the snow. In the road. Shrieking, and waving her arms at the car.

He stopped and came out to her. Bathed in the green-blue mars light of the cruiser. And she was crying and shrieking that her car wouldn't start.

Her car was in the ditch, at a thirty-degree angle, nose pointed up at the sky, the headlights going yellow as the battery died.

The woman was drunk and incoherent, babbling about the car.

"The man," he said. "You said someone was hurt."

"The *hospital,*" she said. "The fucken car died." And she turned toward the car in the ditch.

"Where do you live?" he said. She gestured up the hill, to a farmhouse three hundred yards away. "Get in," he said, and put her in the back of the cruiser, and drove to the house.

The farmhouse door was open, and lights were on. He stood on the porch and called, "Hello . . ." There was no answer. He stepped into the house and saw the body on the floor.

There was blood sprayed over one wall and part of the ceiling. The black automatic lay on the floor, hammer back.

"He was dead as he's ever going to be," he said; "but the *thing* was, I knew she didn't kill 'im. And I *thought* about it, you see, to see how I knew. I couldn't tell you. And I *knew* she didn't kill 'im." He paused.

The girl drew her feet up on the chair, and tugged the t-shirt down over her knees, and hugged her legs to her. The man looked over at the motion, then he looked back, and took up his thought.

*   *   *

Both in the wax and in the wood there were patterns
constantly forming.

The wax dripped off the green iron candlestick and
onto his hand. On the back of his finger it fell hot, and
then very hot; and he tried to reason why it was less hot
at first.

He enjoyed the vacant exercise of trying to apply his
limited knowledge of science; and, when he could not
solve this problem, said to himself, "Well, who, finally,
understands anything anyway?" and lapsed back into
watching the wax drip down the candle, and over the
rim of the candlestick — one drop gliding down over
another. Just when you thought it must fall, it con-
gealed, and made a new and unexpected but inevitable
shape in the wax stalactite.

"Yes," he thought, and unconsciously compared it to
some unnamed comparative, and found the juxtaposi-
tion pleasing and instructive. "Life is like that," he
thought; and it was not that he had found the answer,
but, as in the case of the heated wax, that he had been
calmed, and, for a moment, his brain ceased to strive.

The candle sat on a table to the left of the couch. In
front of him the fire burnt in the open stove.

"And all the logs that I swore I'd remember," he
thought, "though I were to see them a hundred years
on." He smiled, and thought back to the splitting — the
splitting, sweaty shirt, salt in his eyes, and his back ach-
ing; and how he swore at a twisted log that would not
split, or at one he had lost a wedge in; and swore he'd

remember and relive it when it came to throw that log on the fire.

But here it was these months later, and, though he kept a general and pleasant memory of the work and the exercise of splitting; though he remembered his oaths to remember, he could not, of course, recall the individual twisted logs; and, again, his mind tried to fashion a general principle from his observation.

"It's almost as if," he thought. Then a log sputtered in the stove, and sent strange sparks against the screen, as it fell on the bed of ashes.

He walked to the stove, and took a length of apple branch from the kindling pile. He moved the screen, and, with the poker, leaned the fallen log up out of the ashes, and shoved the apple branch underneath it.

He replaced the screen and sat back down. The fire blazed up underneath the log, as the air came to it, and licked up the sides.

"Because it warms you twice," he thought.

It formed into a beast, with fire coming from its mouth. A dog or an alligator. A bird, he thought, if the back part were just a bit more crossways, to let me think it was a wing.

"Well, perhaps it could be a bird in any case," he thought, "if . . ."

It hummed in the stove, and crackled in the most arrhythmic, perfect, soothing progression. Flames shot up from a new place in the top of the log.

"There are people who do not think," he thought. "Animals do not think, and lead their lives one beautiful moment to the next. But this is as close as I can come to it."

*   *   *

"No, it wasn't that long ago," she thought. And, so, what were they talking about?

"Woodcarvers Convention," she read. "*Playgroup.*" Well, hell, it was a short, such a short step from being in, when you thought your parents were hags, old hags, what were they doing? And from taking your kids *to* the playgroup. Leaving them there, all the things they would do.

"Sit in the corner, smoke cig-rettes, talk about the men," she thought.

"Such a short jump. *That* was the basis of the thing. *That* was what they all were talking about, with 'the passage of time.' What the *fuck* did it all mean?"

A young girl came out of the food store. "H'lo, Maris," she said. Maris nodded. "Hm," she said.

"Y'doing . . . ?"

"Looking at this thing," Maris said.

The other girl turned and surveyed the window with her.

". . . is she *looking* at?" Maris thought. "S'if there was something up on the glass would *interest* her." She saw the other girl turn, and try to form a comment, she saw it, like a wave, as if the thought were a wave, out in the ether, and then it was in your head, then it was building in there, and then it *formed,* and put pressure on you, till you had to say it.

" 'How are you doing?' probably," she thought, "or . . ."

". . . you, you, you know . . ." the other girl said, and Maris was surprised to see something out of the commonplace in her face. She waited. "You know," the other girl said, and Maris leaned closer to her. The phone rang. Maris looked shocked. Both of them stood listening to the ringing of the phone, then Maris made a gesture, as if to say, "Well, what the fuck can you *do* . . . ?" and she moved around to the side of the grocery, to the wall phone, and picked it up.

"H'lo . . . ?" she said.

The other girl stayed by the glass front of the store. She looked at the various notices. A bike for sale. Split wood. An auction coming up, The Family and Friends of so-and-so wish to thank, for their kind expression . . .

She heard Maris on the phone.

"Well, I said I would and I will," she said.

"No, I *said* I would, and I *will*," she said again, her voice rising.

The other girl waited, moving off a bit, trying to find that spot which would be far enough from the phone to indicate polite recognition of privacy; but not so far as to convey the impression that she was abandoning the conversation.

She moved to the far side of the grocery door. The notices here were all banners for specials on food.

Maris huddled herself into the small overhang of the wall phone. "*Look*," she said. "*You* called *me* . . ."

"Oh, hell," she said to herself, and began to shake her head, and twist her body side-to-side. Her hand covered the mouthpiece. "Oh, hell," she said, softly. "Oh, hell . . ."

*   *   *

He dreamed he had lost the children. In his dream he had left them on a streetcar in the rain, and hailed a cab, and started home, when he remembered them.

"There is no way," he thought, "that the children will be home when I arrive there. I can wish all I want, but all laws of human behavior, and chance, and cause-and-effect would have to be suspended for the children to be home when I arrive."

And as he dreamt it came to him that there was one way the children might be at home: if it were a dream. And in his dream he recognized that it *was* a dream; and, further, that perhaps many, and perhaps all hopeless misery was subject to this same mechanism in the waking world.

The thought stayed with him all the morning.

"That," he thought, that perhaps God was telling him something; or that a screen had been momentarily lifted, and he'd been allowed a glimpse of the true workings of the inner world.

He went out on the porch, and the soft *thut* of an apple falling turned his head.

The green apples were scattered underneath the tree.

"They get to a point, then they fall," he thought; "what could be more logical than that? Nothing."

And was not his assurance that the children were irremediably gone as sure, as adamantine, as anything in his life? He searched his memory. "Yes," he thought. "Yes." For it required a system of understanding that he did not possess, even to hope for their return. But on the appearance of that system, "of that mechanism," he thought, the hopeless was instantly transformed into the sure.

Another apple thudded on the ground. His head turned to see it rolling half a foot, two feet, down the gentle slope from the base of the tree.

"But there are limits," he thought. "If the apple — if the 'base' of the stem," he thought, pleased with the precision of his reason, ". . . if the base of the stem, which has been engineered to be that which parts first . . ." He shaded his eyes against the morning sun, and looked on, past the apple tree, and down the field to the pond.

"If the forces of nature are conjoined to *rot* it; and to rot it *first,* so that it *separates* from the tree, what intercession could there be? Who would want to suspend all natural laws, to cause the stem to adhere past the time when . . .

"Aha. Aha . . ." he thought. "The apple is part of the larger system. It would be manifestly ludicrous for the one apple to adhere interminably, when the tree had all gone bare. And the *difference* must be," he thought, "the *difference* must be, that the *apple,*" he thought, "that . . ." The screen door slammed, and he turned to see his wife.

She sat on the porch step, facing ninety degrees away from him. "Up early," she said. He nodded the back of his head toward her. "Hard night?" she said.

"What can she want?" he thought. He turned partly toward her.

"There is another way to look at this," he thought.

"And this is what it is: that billions and billions of atoms have collided and adhered, momentarily, into this form, which we know as The World. . . . And also, *also*," he thought, "into this form *which is our consciousness. And* . . ." He felt as if in the epiphany of his dream, as if some unexpected vista were opening before him. It was a physical feeling, as in the first recognition of a fever breaking, or the first sign of the true end of an oppressive heat wave.

"*And*," he thought.

"Well, I need the big car today," she said.

"No," he thought. "No. The interruption doesn't matter, because . . ."

"I have to go to Bradford."

". . . because . . ." he thought.

". . . and I know you said . . ."

He prayed that he could shut her out, and was delighted to find that he could. Her voice was gone, and he, as if reimmersed in a long-sought sleep, was engrossed once more in his thought.

"Because," he thought. ". . . because . . ."; and he was lost and abandoned. Neither the specifics nor the trend of his thought remained to him.

"No. It's going," he thought. "It's going."

". . . and that's why I ask you now," her voice said. He turned to face her.

"That's why now."

He saw her look in wondering at him, and thought he detected fear in her look, and he liked it.

"What," she said, ". . . what's wrong with you?"

"What's wrong with me?" He said, "I was thinking of something."

"Well. Thinking of something. Well. You might give me your attention," she said.

He turned back toward the apple tree. ". . . don't you think?" she said. "*Henry,*" she said, and paused. "*Henry,*" she said. "Don't you think?"

"Don't I think what?"

"She has the same problem as me," he thought; "she can't remember what the fuck she was thinking of."

"Don't you *think,*" she said, her voice full and sure, "that you might do me the *courtesy* of paying me polite *attention,*" she said, "when I am *addressing* you?"

On the far side of the pond he saw a shape that did not belong there. "Ah," he thought. It was a small patch of grey-brown in not quite the right shade to be the dried grass. It was a deer. And as he looked, it moved. It was the front shoulder of a deer. She raised her head, and the patch that he had been looking at became her shoulder.

Her head came up, and she moved a few feet, and lowered her head again to browse, blending into the landscape.

Six

The day was not hot and it was not cold.

He put a light wool vest over his t-shirt, and felt clammy in the thick humidity. He removed it and was cold.

"It will be warm when I start work," he thought.

He heard the screen door slam, and looked up to see his wife, walking down from the porch to the car.

He stood in the shade of the barn door, and watched, sure she could not see him, as she slid into the seat, adjusted the mirrors, then started the engine and backed out into the road and started down to Town. He walked back to the barn, holding his vest in his hand.

There were small, shallow bays, formed by the two-by-six uprights framing the inside of the barn wall. Nails and hooks in the walls and in the uprights held tools, gardening clothes, and equipment. In one bay cross-country skis hung on pegs, perpendicular to the ground. And in the next bay there was a maul, leaning, head down on the ground, handle up against the upright.

Next to it, on the ground, lay two metal wedges, one with traces of red paint on it, the other with traces of green. Above them, on a shelf, lay the cleaned and oiled chainsaw.

He slipped the vest on. He took the wedges in one hand, and the maul in the other, and walked out of the barn.

Up past the house was the woodpile — ten cord of hardwood he'd cut into 24-inch lengths.

The ground around the pile was deep in chips. The chips were dark from the previous day's rain, and they gave off a wet smell.

He walked to the pile, and looked around for a conspicuous place to put the wedges. The grey, scarred sawbuck was on its side on the ground. He righted it, and rested the maul against it, and laid the wedges underneath. He turned around, and there was the piece he'd sawed out for the chopping block.

It was a butt of maple a foot and a half high, and a foot and a half across. He walked to it and kicked the chips from the area near it, where he would put his feet. He heard a car on the road, and turned to watch it, for a moment, as it drove down the road.

He went to the sawbuck. He took it in one hand, and the maul handle in the other, and put them five feet to the right of the chopping block. He stood facing the block, the woodpile just behind him to his left. He walked to it and chucked several length of wood log toward the block. He picked up another length and carried it back, and set it on the block. He turned the check in the wood to face him.

He stepped to the sawbuck. He reached in the back pocket of his pants and took out a pair of worn, yellow cowhide gloves. He drew the gloves on. He took off his hat, and hung it on a corner of the sawbuck.... He picked up the maul and stood in front of the chopping block again, and looked at the check in the wood — a dark radius, starting just inside the bark and pointing at the heart of the wood.

He started to heft the maul, then stopped. He put the maul down. He looked back over the area, out in the brown woodchips, where the sawbuck had been. He saw the glint of the green and the red of the two wedges.

He fetched them and put them down next to the chopping block.

He scuffed his feet on the ground to make sure they were clear; he raised the maul over his head, and looked at the check in the wood.

"Chop to the *block*," he said to himself. "Chop right through the wood."

The maul came down and he felt as if, before the maul reached it, the wood split in two clean halves. One half fell off the block, leaving the other half standing upright. He turned that piece back toward him, and raised the maul over his head. "Chop for the block," he said to himself.

He worked on, and the pile of split wood grew behind the chopping block. The back of his neck, and his shoulders were warmed by the work, and felt liquid and good. Once in a while he would put a gnarled and knotted log on the block and when he'd split it — using the wedges, usually — he'd look at the convoluted grain he'd revealed, and, as he tossed it on the pile, he'd grin and he knew he'd remember that piece, which had given him such trouble, when the time came to stack it. And he thought, too, that he'd remember it in the Winter, when he'd taken it from the shed, to burn in the stove.

"It warms you three times," he thought. "They say it warms you when you cut it, and it warms you when you burn it; but I think it also warms you when you *look* at it all cut and split and stacked." Then he felt ashamed of his thoughts for a moment, almost as if he had voiced them to some group, which shamed him for what he thought of as his sentimentality.

And all the time he chopped the wood. Sometimes he'd use the wedge, reversing the maul to strike it down into the wood. And sometimes a wedge would lodge deep in the wood, and he'd have to turn the piece and use the other wedge to split the first one out.

Once, several years before, down in the Village, at the Store, he'd suggested that sometimes the wood might split before the maul had even reached it. And the men, politely, he thought, responded that it might be a trick of the light; or, perhaps it was effected, if it was, by compression of air, like a sonic boom, or like a ship's bow-wave. Or they understood him to be speaking figuratively, and they indicated that.

But then he persisted that it seemed to him not poetry at all, nor science, as he understood it, nor fantasy, but, in truth, a fact — that, sometimes, the piece split of itself, before the maul reached it, as if his relaxed and focused intention were enough to split it. When he so persisted, he saw their reaction, and retreated, without sharing his other observation about splitting wood.

He heard her car crunch up, as it slowed in the gravel of the road. He saw it turn onto the drive and stop. The engine was cut off, and her door opened.

"Yep," he thought, "and, all the same, it's true. And if you say 'I've got to lay the maul'. . ." As he rehearsed his perception to himself, on the word "maul," he brought the maul down on a piece of wood. The two halves flew away.

He reached back to his left, and grabbed another chunk, and lifted it onto the block. Unconsciously now, he turned it to show the best face for splitting, and raised the maul over his head, using, always, his rhythm, and the weight of the objects, rather than his strength, whenever he could.

" '. . . the *maul*,' " he thought, as he raised it over his head, " 'directly *in* the check . . .' " he thought, and, on the word "check," brought it down.

The head lodged in the wood. And he levered it out, and raised it once again.

" 'Directly *in* the check,' " he thought, and brought the maul down. Once again, the head stuck. He nodded, and levered it out of the wood.

He pushed the wood off the chopping block and sat on the block, the maul head on the ground, the handle leaning on the outside of his thigh.

His right hand absently reached in his vest pocket for a cigarette. Then he looked up to the sawbuck, where he had hung his vest. He stepped over to it, through the small field of split wood, lying clean, white, and naked in a tumble on the ground.

"No artist could do this," he thought. He took a cigarette from the pack in his vest, and turned back to look at the wood. "No artist could do it," he thought. "It's too various." He lit a match on his khaki pants, drawing his thigh up to make the pants seat taut. He smelt the sulfur, and the smallest whiff of burnt fabric. He smelled the still-fragrant woodchips, and the last bit of dew on them and on the grass. He lit his cigarette and drew the smoke in. He rubbed the back of his neck and smiled.

He heard the screen door slam; and, moments later, the car's engine start again.

The maul handle rested against the chopping block. He sat on the block, moving the handle out of the way. As he sat, it levered back and rested again against his thigh.

The squirrel ran across the road, and "you could not tell," he thought, "in both the shape and the rhythm of the thing, if it was a squirrel or a fallen leaf blowing across the road.

"As many times," he thought, "as many times as I've seen it, you never can tell. And *why*," he thought; "what would it *benefit* to have the one mimic the other? The squirrel runs across the road, and *goddamn*, if, the way he stops and starts, it doesn't look just like . . ."

He saw her walking down the road, and knew from her gait that she knew someone was looking at her, and felt also that she somehow knew that it was him. "Without turning around," he thought.

He slowed the truck and pulled level with her. She looked over, still walking. "Maris . . ." he said. The truck and the girl moved on at her walking pace.

"Get *in*," he said. "Going down to Town?"

"Why does that sound so foolish?" he thought. "Where the sick hell would she be going down to?"

"Down to Town," she said. "Isn't that the sole place this fucken road goes?" She stopped walking, and he stopped the truck.

"C'n I get *in* . . . ?" she said, and walked around and got into the cab.

Dick started the truck down the road. Driving as slowly as he could, without, as he thought, drawing attention to the fact.

"No. The point is not to go fast or slow," he thought, "but to drive *carefully*." He saw her out of the corner of his eye.

"Cold for today," he said.

"What?" she said.

"Cold for today." She looked back at the road and smiled.

"How can it be 'cold' for today . . . ?"

"Your, your . . ." he said, ". . . your *clothes* are cold for . . ."

"My *clothes* . . . ?" she said.

"I meant that you're lightly dressed," he said.

She rubbed her face with her left hand, wearily; as if he were the last of an afternoon of foolish petitioners.

They drove on down the winding dirt road. The beautiful trees were already starting to thin, and patches of orange and yellow were seen through the green.

"*Maris,*" he said. "Do you ever think about *mimicry?*" he said, proud of the word.

"What in the fuck do you want?" she said.

He was stunned. He looked at her and realized he'd pulled the truck over and stopped.

"What the *fuck* are you talking about?"

". . . I . . ." he started to say.

"*What?*"

He heard the big engine gearing down, and looked up to see the huge log truck coming up the hill. He raised a finger to the driver, to say "just a minute, I'll move it," and pulled his pickup far over on the right shoulder. The big log carrier inched by on his left side. He looked in his outside mirror, and saw the driver's face, reflected in the other mirror, as the man checked the clearance between the two trucks. The big, stake-sided carrier, empty of logs, swayed a bit as it cleared the pickup, and then the driver accelerated up the hill.

"M'always *afraid* on this road," he said, "one've those things, going to come loose, when it's coming at you, break loose in the rain, and swing around in *front* of you." He looked at her. She nodded her head once, as if to accept what she understood to be his obeisance and confession. He cleared his throat.

"Bad day today?" he said.

"Something like that," she said, low. They sat for a moment, then she looked at the road; then she looked at him and raised her eyebrows.

He put the pickup in gear and started back down the road.

As he drove, the silence built again, till he found himself concentrating on his driving; as if he had never seen the road before and it was impossibly dangerous. "What the hell am I thinking about?" he thought, and found that he was swinging wide on the right turn, and it was not impossible that he would drift off into the ditch. He geared down, and corrected, and made the turn, just barely staying on the road.

"What the hell is *wrong* with me?" he thought. The road seemed strange as he tried to cast his mind ahead to the next turn. "How far is it to Town?" he thought. "This is impossible. It's as if I'd forgotten my wife's *name* . . ."

"There is a turn to the *left*, then the short straight stretch above the ravine, where we always see that doe, and then . . ."

"Bobby Dole, getting up the hill, back to his *wife*, up there," she said.

"What?" he said. "Yes. That's right." And took her words for an apology; or, at the least, for an invitation to converse.

"Bobby Dole," he said. "Goin' up to his wife." He made a clucking sound in his teeth. "Takin' the rig home."

"You ever want to do that?" he said. "Get in the *woods* — work *outside* all day?" She shrugged her shoulder up to her left ear.

". . . stuck in the *store* all the time . . ." he said, and made an "offering" gesture toward her, as if to say,

"That, of course, is a response *you* might make. To what I've said. Consider that I've made it for you, and no offence . . ."

". . . stuck in the *store*," he said. ". . . *orders . . . inventory . . .*" He jollied himself along, as if he'd found his true audience.

"Not very *romantic*," he said. He found that he was down on the flat, just beyond the Town, and was surprised and pleased he'd managed the drive.

"But now," he thought, "now I'm speaking to her *naturally*, but now we're almost *there . . .*"

". . . get off at the bridge," she said.

". . . waal, that's *right*," he said, and wondered, as the words left his mouth, what they might mean. "And how's things at *your* house?" And she turned and looked at him with a mixture of warning and contempt.

"Yep," he thought. "Well, the world goes on." He pulled the pickup over by the bridge. She opened the door and got out.

"Thank you," she said, closing the door.

He drove over the bridge, and turned onto the hardtop road. As he did, he looked in the mirror. "I have *done* that," he thought, "to check traffic." He saw her walking on to the porch of the house, then his view of her was wiped out by the bridge.

"And this and that," her mother said. "But don't you fucken tell me you were out *working*, or *looking* for work, or out with your *friends*, or out doing anything but what I *know* you were doing, because I can't stand the disrespect."

Maris stood there and glared at her.

"And, now, if you want to *do* something, go *do* it, and leave off *staring* at me. What you think that will accomplish, I don't know.

"Now, I've been waiting for you, and you can go to the store, and get some bread and milk and half a pound *hamburger,* and get down there. If you would."

"Store's closed," the girl said.

"Store is *not* closed, and I'll thank you to do as I ask."

Maris walked to the door, and reached around it. She found her heavy flannel shirt, by touch, on the hook. In the next room she saw the man, in the rocking chair, looking out the window.

"Well, the fuck *could* look at me," she thought. "What is *he* playing at?" She walked to the front door, shaking her head.

She went up the road, to the bridge, fighting her way into the large flannel shirt.

". . . I'd like to *do* to him," she thought, "I'd like to get him somewhere. Off the road, coming home some night, force him right off the road. He gets out — maybe he's drunk, I don't care — I don't give a shit, sober or drunk, he gets out. Something with hitting. He bends down, I hit him with a tire iron, a *crowbar,* something, maybe he turns around, in the last minute, and I see it in his face. As he turns around. The last second. He's thinking, 'Why me? Everyone *likes* me. Isn't it unfair?' I hope.

"And then I got him with his head stove in, and drag him back into the woods. I wish I had a cabin, or something back there, with a hole in it. Or some abandoned *mine.* And I'd have him back there. And chain him to some *logs* or something, or some framework they had there, to keep the mineshaft up. And keep him where no one could hear him scream. And I'd keep him down there. Until he *whimpered.*"

She stopped on the bridge, and slowed her breathing. She felt tall, and resolute, and indomitable. She felt as if her gaze would deter any chance aggression.

"For he'd think I would relent," she thought. "Then he's wrong." She walked onto the blacktop, and turned toward the store.

"There he is wrong," she thought; "that stupid *fuck* — to think I would be turned by his, what? By his suffering . . . ? 'That's what I *brought* you for!' " she said to him in her thoughts.

"That is why you're *here.* Don't you know that your cries for pity are my sweetest *sounds?*" she'd say. And then she'd tire of the mere mental pain of worry she'd been subjecting him to, and she would torture him.

"I'm going to give you a choice," she would say. "He thinks," she thought, "that I am just toying with him again, but this time he's going to be wrong."

"Which would you like?" she'd say. "I will put out your eyes, or cut your *dick* off. You have four seconds to choose. And if you don't choose, I will do both."

She liked this plan because she reasoned that given more time than the four seconds, the man might attempt to "psychologize" her, as she put it to herself.

"Give 'im more time," she thought, "he might reason that I'd do to him the thing he liked least, so if he chose to give up his *eyes,* I'd likely take the *other* thing. But *no,* you fucking cocksucker," she thought, though still, in her imagination, within the grace period of the four seconds.

"You fucking cocksucker," she thought, and, in her thoughts, picked up a large, wickedly sharp knife, and began to slash him across his face.

"What are you *screaming* for?" she thought. "Don't you *like* it . . . ?"

"Were you *mistaken* in me, you stupid shit?"

She passed the window of the hardware store, and saw Dick, elbows on the counter, talking to Mrs. Bell. Out of the corner of her eye, she saw Dick steal a glance at her, as he continued talking. But she saw, by his and Mrs. Bell's change in demeanor, that they had begun talking about her.

"The lot of you," she thought. "Ears back like jackasses."

Inside the food store James was switching the lights off.

Maris stepped up and into the store.

"Closing, Maris," he said.

"Three things," Maris said.

"All right," he said.

Seven

The old man opened the canvas bag and took the jacket out.

The jacket was some light, grey quilted material, some early synthetic.

It was frayed at the two slash pockets, and frayed at the collar and cuffs. He pulled the jacket on, fastened the snaps, and put his red wool hunting coat on over it.

He dug into a pocket of the red coat, and brought out an olive-drab canvas hat. The hat had a floppy brim, and a hatband of olive-drab elastic loops.

He put the hat on. Henry looked at him and thought, "What could they have been for? A lighter? Cigarettes? Not shells, certainly, for who would want to keep shells around his head . . . ? What else? A compass . . . ?"

He tried to cast his imagination back to the battlefield of the Second World War, for the hat was obviously of that vintage, and the fabric of the hat, that was its era.

Henry looked at the man. He wanted to ask him.

And ask if he had fought in the War, as he was sure he had.

He thought that he saw something in the man's bearing; or, more certainly, in the impulse that had caused him to keep the hat, these fifty years. "It must be so deep," Henry thought, "that it must be associated with combat.

"He has a face like that. That Yankee Face," he thought.

Lynn reached down and put one arm through the strap of the canvas bag, and slung the bag up behind him. He picked up his shotgun, broke it open, and carried it in the crook of his left elbow. He looked at Henry. "Ready?" he said.

"Yes, I am," Henry said; and they walked off, down the lane.

The lane had been a road one hundred years before. It was some twenty feet across, and bordered on either side by low, laid stone walls. Beyond the walls were once farm fields. But the fields were many decades gone, and the woods grew up to the stone walls.

The dog would romp before them ten or twenty yards; then she would look back at her master, and wait for a moment, as the men walked closer up. Then she would run forward again.

"Fine day for it," Henry said.

"Couldn't imagine a better," Lynn said. He reached his right hand behind him, into the canvas sack, and brought out two red shotgun shells. He turned slightly to Henry, to show he was loading his gun. Henry nodded, to say that he noted it. He took two shells from his pocket, and the men loaded their shotguns.

Up ahead the dog turned and she quieted. The breeches of the guns clapped closed, one after the other.

The men moved farther apart on the lane, and slowed the pace of their walk. The dog waited as the men walked up on her, then stepped to the old man, who held the gun in his right hand for a second, as he gestured to the dog. He swept his left hand low and out and forward to say, "That's right. *Go*, now. Go do it."

The dog trotted away, forward. Ahead, yellow sunlight shone on a patch of the lane. There was a break in the wall, and a natural clearing beyond it. The dog went into the clearing. The two men followed her, Henry going to the left, and the old man to the right, after the dog.

They slowly worked their way around the edges of the clearing, circling against each other.

Henry walked, his thumb on the shotgun safety, always expecting the *thutter* of the rising bird.

The two men convened at the clearing's far side, where the dog sat waiting, patiently and curious, for the men who did not know there were no birds there.

They passed through a small stand of white pine, even with each other, thirty feet apart, moving quietly on the rust-colored needles.

Off to the right the dog flushed a bird.

Out of the corner of his eye Henry saw the old man mount the gun, and start to swing to his left, after the bird. Henry turned his head with the gun, saw the bird, and his own gun was on his shoulder, and the safety off, as the bird got up, darted his way, and dove into the woods.

Neither man had shot. Henry lowered his gun, and looked around to where the other man had done the same. The old man smiled at him. Henry smiled back. Then they both started out again.

"And what did the ass see, that the man did *not* see? Well, he saw an *angel.* He saw the angel. With the sword. In the midst of the road. Barring his way. Do you see? Barring Balaam's way, and do you know what I mean when I say 'willfulness'? What is willfulness?"

None of the children raised a hand. "Yes. It is a big word." He smiled.

"It means, simply, to do something because you want to. Whether it's right or wrong. Whether your friends, or parents, or *teachers,*" he made a small, self-deprecatory bow, "advise you not to. To *continue* in a path *just because* you think it is right. How many know Doc?" Some of the children raised their hands.

"Well, of *course* you do," he said. "Of course you do. Now: here's a story. Back in the Horse and *Buggy* days — this is a story his uncle told him. Yes, Frank?"

"Who was his uncle?"

"His uncle was *also* a doctor. Doctor Holt. Who died before you, before I was born. He was a doctor, long ago."

"Just like Doc."

"Well, it was his *uncle* . . ."

"In the Civil War . . . ?"

The minister stopped. He thought, "Died in, well, before Doc went to War; so, died in, what? Forty?

Thirty? Forty the latest, s'even at the age of eighty, if he was . . ."

"No," he said. "In the period just after the Civil War. And, in those days, there were no automobiles. And the *Doctor* got around on horse and buggy.

"Now, you know the bridge up by the quarry?"

The boys nodded, and the girls looked at each other.

"Coming home one night. Such a dark night. Rain storm. In the Spring. Heavy rain. Asleep. Do you see? Old Doc was asleep. Been up all night, some farmhouse, and now coming home. He was asleep as the *horse* knew the *way*." He stopped and rubbed his thumb and forefinger on either side of his mouth, several times.

"The *horse* knew the way back, and it was so dark, in the rain, you could not see your hand, if you held it in *front* of you." One of the boys did so, and the Minister said, "Yes. That's how dark it was. He'd fallen *asleep,* and . . ." Several other boys now held their hands out in front of their face. One of them closed his eyes, and tried to squint through them. The Minister continued.

". . . *woken* by the sound of the horse stopping, and he knew, by the sound, that the horse had stopped on the quarry bridge. He *woke,* and looked out over the bridge, but he could not see over it. And he clucked to the horse, '*giddap!*' " he said, and was happy with the touch. "You know? To urge him on? And the horse did not want to go, but stepped out, one step, two steps, on the planks of the bridge — yes, I know," he said, "but *in those days,* it was made of wood. Then it was a *wooden* bridge, and the horse stepped out on it, just those two steps, and then would not move. And Doc was tired, and wet, and angry. But the horse would not move, and nothing could force him to go out upon that bridge. Do you know . . ." A boy shot his hand up.

"Yes, Arthur?"

"The bridge was out," the boy said.

"That's ab — " Another boy put his hand up.

"No, Arthur is, no, the bridge *was* out. The bridge was washed out. Halfway across. The rain washed it out. Way in the middle, past, *way* past what the man could have seen. Or what the *horse* could . . ." He cleared his throat. "What the *horse* could see.

"Now, here's a vision of a man. Wet, cold, and *angry. You'd* be angry, too. Wouldn't you? Middle of the night, you want to get home . . . ? And, perhaps he *whipped* the horse. But *That Horse,* which he thought so ignorant, saved that man's life. For, if they'd gone out on that *bridge,* they would have died. Yes. Frank?"

"How did the horse know?"

"How did the horse know that the bridge was out," the Minister said.

"Yes."

"We don't know."

"Was it Extrasensory Perception?"

"We don't know." He walked around, and sat on the front of the desk. There was a pause, and each of the children looked toward his best friend.

Softly, the Minister said, as if to himself, not to break the mood, "We do not know."

"And, had he *died,* do you see?" he continued, "Had he *died? . . .*" He paused. "Had he *Died . . .*" He stopped again, caught up as much in his own rhythm as in his thoughts. He looked out of the window. "A white day," he thought. He heard the children begin to talk tentatively to each other.

"What kept the horse on the bridge?" he thought. "How many of these stories are simply coincidence? Not *all* of them . . ."

He turned back and saw the two boys debating earnestly, softly, and the one shaking his head. The boy put his hand up.

"Yes?" the Minister said.

"Did they do tests on him?"

". . . tests," he said, and thought, " 'Tests,' what does he mean?"

"Tests. Tests on the horse?"

"Yes," the boy said.

"I don't believe so," the Minister said. "Now."

He got down from the desk and walked to the blackboard. Five words were written, one over the other, and he pointed to the third of them. "Now," he said.

The birds were on the table. Skin, feathers, and innards were in an old metal can, on the floor by the side.

The man cleared his throat. He wiped his hands with a grey dishtowel, and took the large, one-bladed pocket knife from his pants pocket, opened it, and wiped the blade on the dishtowel. He held the knife in one hand and rested the blade on the thumbnail of his other hand. He jiggled the knife minutely, and the blade skittered to one side of the thumbnail, and he nodded, as if to say "I thought so."

He gestured to the bottle, and Henry poured them each another shot.

The man opened the drawer in the table, and removed an oblong whetstone, set into a block of wood. He took a small can of gun oil out of the drawer, and pushed the drawer shut.

He looked around, and reached across the table to a glass-based Kerosene lamp, and pulled the lamp to him. He took off the lamp's glass chimney, put it aside, then unscrewed the brass burner. The long wick dripped kerosene on the table, as he put the burner aside.

He took a green bandanna from his pants pocket, and dipped it in the kerosene in the lamp base. He scrubbed the whetstone with the bandanna, until the grey stone started to look clean.

He screwed the lamp back together, and looked at the bandanna, which now was black with grit and with oil. He put it back in his pocket.

He opened the can of gun oil and squirted oil on the stone.

He used his index finger to move the coat of oil smoothly over it. He wiped his hand on the tail of his flannel shirt.

He picked the pocketknife up, and he held it so the bevel of its edge glinted in the late afternoon sun. He began whetting the knife — five strokes on one side, then five on the other.

"The great thing is, of course, the deer," he said.

"The great thing is, I always found, when it comes down to you better of practiced, because, when you *see* 'im, you will, of course, have no time at all."

"Well, *if* you see 'im . . ." Henry said.

"They're out there," Lynn said. "You have to get out there and get an education." The man took the knife and wiped the blade on his pants. He looked at the table, and, not seeing what he wanted, patted his pockets.

Henry felt in his shirt pocket, and brought out the shopping list. He held it deferentially toward the old man, as if to say, "I assume this is what you need; but I don't mean to offend by anticipating you."

Lynn took it, and gently drew the knife blade over the paper's edge. The knife sliced the paper, and the man smiled. He put a drop of oil on each side of the blade, wiped it off on his pants, and closed the knife and dropped it into his pants pocket.

The fire in the woodstove cracked. The man drank his bourbon, rose, walked to the stove, and spat on it. The spit balled and skittered across the stove top. The man went to the wall and took down an old, black, cast-iron saucepan. He took it to the table, and began to prepare to cook the birds.

The cabin smelled of the lamp oil, woodsmoke, and the smell of the game.

Lynn seasoned the birds, in the falling darkness, in the kitchen.

Henry gestured toward the lamp, and Lynn nodded at him, and Henry lit the lamp.

It was going quickly dark outside, and the kerosene lamp on the table was the only light.

Henry leant his chair back against the wall. He saw the deep orange glow from the grate in the cookstove. The fire popped. He eased his chair down, and leaned forward to the table. He stubbed his cigarette out in the tin can ashtray, and took another from the pack lying there.

The bottle was almost done. He reached carefully for it, and his glass, and poured out what he approximated was one-half of the remainder.

The old man was sitting across the table from him. His heels were propped on the windowsill, which also held the whiskey glass. There was a cigarette cupped in the left hand that lay relaxed in his thigh.

Henry looked at him a moment, then raised himself in stages, and stood by the table. He picked up his glass, and drank the last drop in it. He took his coat from the back of his chair and got into it.

He glanced at his watch, and looked at it for a while; then picked a wooden match up off the table and lit it.

The man turned at the sound. Henry nodded, and moved to the cabin door.

" 'Night, Henry," the man said.

" 'Night, Lynn," he said.

"Well, hell," Marty said, "there are good days, and there's *bad* days, and that's just the way it is." He paused. "And if you were never *down*, how'd you know when you were up . . . ?" He looked and he could see that he wasn't making an impression. "Y'expect to have luck in *everything?* You're lucky in so much. Now: you n'Judy, that's good luck . . . this . . . this . . ." He paused.

"Years go by, and you'll *laugh* at shit like this. Though, I can see, p'raps that's not the greatest consolation." He sighed. He looked at his son and he shrugged. "S'many troubles in the world." He lowered his eyes. "N'when you think ... when you think ... Awright," he said, "g'wan." The boy started to get up slowly, respectfully, rising from the couch with a suggestion of reluctance, or of serious consideration for what he had heard.

"But one more thing: there is no shame in *losing*," his father said. "That is the *worst* sin — to tell somebody that." He shook his head. "All of the *nonsense* that you hear, that is the *worst* sin, s'm'y, wants to live his life through you, 'you've disappointed me,' you tell that man ..." He chewed the inside of his lip, shaking his head, his eyes seeing something far away. John felt it, and turned, and looked at him, concerned; then Marty took a deep intake of breath, and turned and looked at his son.

"All kinds of fools in the world. *Most* of them are going to try, blame it on *you*. Watch if they don't. Full of fools. Thieves, cheats, motherfuckers, like that man at the *high school*, n'I'm talking to you straight, cause I want you to understand. Most Of What You Find In This Life's going to be *failure*, of one sort, another.

"... Understand? Because that is the nature of life.

"Politicians, *lawyers* ... ;" He gestured, to indicate, "as in the case-at-hand," "people in *authority* ... Now: many times: you have to listen to their shit. But you do not have to believe it.

"You hear me, son ... ?"

He looked at the boy, and saw that his words had come home and made a difference. He debated several endings to his speech, and various instructions, or suggestions. "You go to the practice, now, and *tell* that son of a bitch . . ."; or, "My suggestion is to act with the pride which you have, and act as though nothing had . . ."

But he saw that John was thinking, and the correct end of the lesson was to let him do so. So he patted the boy on the cheek, and nodded, to say, "Well, that's all." He went back to the kitchen table, and took up his magazine.

Out of the corner of his eye he saw the boy pull on the heavy coat, and take up his gym bag, and start out the door.

The wind came in with that wet, almost milky aftertaste of snow. Marty patted the paper, to get a good fold, and folded it smartly over to the new page. "Well, all right," he thought. "That son of a bitch."

"Then she asked me what *causes* it," The Trooper said.

"Well, it's a *disease*," the other cop said, and picked up his beer. "What *causes* it . . . ?" he said. "What causes *anything*? Their *body* . . . their *body* has lost the *ability* to . . ." He moved his head from one shoulder to the other, like a railroad crossing signal. ". . . to assimilate," he said, "some fucking thing or other." He picked up his beer and took a swig.

". . . and I was sure the husband's out there," the Trooper said.

"*Can't* be too sure," said the other cop. "Remedial *training*, some instructor, th'academy: some rookie: 'In a fight, how many times should I shoot him?' The Instructor: 'Son, you shoot him till you hear your weapon click empty.' Well, that's fine, n'then you turn around, n'there's his *partner* . . ." He shook his head. "*Never* be too sure."

"And didn't he beat her good," the Trooper said.

"Yup," the other cop said. "I suppose they'd had a disagreement."

"Well, I'll *tell* you," the Trooper said, and the men at the table nodded, as if that said it all.

"*Diabetes*," the other cop said, as if that clinched it, and the three men sat and drank at the table, in the back of the bar.

"This fucken *girl* . . ." the third man said, and his companions gave their attention, turning slightly to him, to acknowledge the introduction of the new topic. The second man turned to the Trooper, who said, "Yuh," to indicate he was acquainted, if not with the girl in question, at least with the man's involvement with her; and that he recognized such as an identifiable and legitimate object of conversation. ". . . and my *wife*," he continued.

"Waal, who forced you to *marry* her?" the second man said.

"True enough," the third man said, and shook his head.

"Ny'way: Ny'way," he said. "I'm out with . . ." He gestured to indicate "the Person under Discussion, whose name I have yet to introduce." "N'she says, 'When will I see you again?' N'I say, excusing myself . . ."

"... uh huh ..." The second man said.

" 'Waal. Next *week.* I'm *busy.*' "

" 'What are you *doing?*' she says. And I am all ready to get hinckty, between, 'none of your business,' and a *lie,* or 'I'll be with my *family.*' But I say, as much out of ..."

"... uh huh," the second man said.

"*Spite,* or something," the man said, " 'I'm going hunting.' And now don't she *smile* and say 'have a good time.' I'm looking for the 'crack in the wall' ... what do they say?"

"The crack in the facade," the second man said.

" 'Crack in the Facade,' " he said, "and damn if she ain't happy that I'm going hunting. No. She's happy. And *I* say: 'Wait a second. Wait a second. You don't think it's somehow *remiss* of me. To want to go *hunting?*' 'Nope,' she says. 'All right,' I say. 'Now: You don't think it's somehow a *sign.* That I'm cov'ring something *up,* about some "doubts" about myself, or something?' "

"You said that?" The Trooper said.

" '... about my "masculinity"?' And she says, 'Well, I like to garden,' which she does, 'do you think that's some sign I doubt my femininity?' she says."

"Well, knock me down with a feather," the second man said.

"... and the *thing,*" the third man said, "that I ..."

"Uh huh," the second man said.

"... find so *surprising:* that the girl *said* that."

"... and she *means* it," the second man said.

"... I know that she does. And the *second* thing is, and this is my question. Isn't it *true,* fine as this girl is,

n'with the most understanding *comment* that I've ever
heard, that if I was to leave my *wife* for her, next deer
season, *wouldn't* she be the one to say, 'Where do you
think you're going?' "

"That's true, too," the second man said.

"Hell of a fucken fucked-up world," the third man
said. "I b'lieve I'll have a drink. *Bill?*"

The Trooper looked up. "Oh, *yuh* . . ." he said.

"Wouldn't be so bad," the second man said, "you
could *understand* it. Could we get a *drink* here?" He
waved to the waitress by the bar, who looked at them
and smiled.

"Yessir," the second Trooper said, commenting on
her.

"Entire *country* . . ." his friend said.

". . . you gents like? 'Nother round?" The waitress
called.

"Yes. We would," the second man said, and smiled
at her.

"Mucked-up to a fare-thee-well," the third man
said. And the three sat silently for half a minute which
each might describe as 'lost in my thoughts,' but which
was only another way to enjoy each others' company.

". . . you boys doin' w'th'criminal elements?" The
waitress said, as she put a new glass in front of each man.

"Doing fine," the second Trooper said.

"Still workin' on it," the third man said; as she
reached to clear the empty beer glass in front of him. She
smiled.

"Now, y'all go home to your wives and your sweet-
hearts," she said.

"Got the order wrong," the second man said. She shook her head, miming disapproval. The Trooper downed his drink, looked at his watch and stood.

"Well . . ." he said. He took the bar napkin from under the empty glass, and wiped his lips. He reached in his back pants pocket and the second man put his hand on the Trooper's arm. "Money's no good here tonight," he said. "You buy tomorrow night."

"Thank you, Tom," the Trooper said.

"Nothing to it."

"Bill, you have a good night, wherever you're *going,* or wherever you happen to *be,*" the third man said.

". . . *Bobby,*" the Trooper said.

"Diabetes, and it smells like shit," the third man said.

The Trooper repositioned his off-duty gun in the holster beneath his short jacket. He walked toward the door.

"Night, hon," the waitress said, and he turned back to her.

"Night, now," he said.

"Night, Bill," the second man called from the table. The Trooper waved back as he walked through the door.

Out in the parking lot, his pickup truck sat under the lamp. He stood on the concrete stoop and zipped up his jacket. He looked at his truck. He stuck his thumb in his mouth, and tore off a small piece of thumbnail. He spat it out onto the gravel, and walked to his truck.

Eight

"Everything changes. It is either growing, or it is dying. And I'm going to tell you that it's not your choice. You might say: 'Then let me be ever-*growing*, Lord, to give myself to Thee,' or something of that sort. Or 'Let me make that choice.' But the choice is not yours, it's not yours to say which portion of the cycle you might be in.

"Let me tell you how you might be deceived. How might you be deceived? In these *times*, do you see? Loss of a *job*, a *death*, a *divorce*, where, to *you*, do you see, the world seems impossible, and your life at an end.

"By no *stretch* of imagination can you see it or feel it as other than death. But how many times in our life, looking back at that pain, have we seen it was *birth* pains. Birth pains. That's right; and those of you who have seen a *woman*, who have been blessed, to see a woman giving birth — and those of you who've given birth — and you know what I'm talking of when you say, as it starts to happen, 'No'; and 'I didn't remember it would be this bad'; and 'I didn't know it would be this bad. Not *this*, Lord. Anything but this. Take it away. Although I wished for it. Take it away. This is not what I meant. Take it away.' And it was giving new life.

"And how many of us. Have stood by the bed, when a loved one, when a friend, so close to death, has fought death — when we knew it was a blessing, and it would release them from their pain. And we stood by that bed. How could we help them, but to wish them peace. And God was sending peace. And yet they fought it. As it is our nature to fight. To resist. To confuse death with life, and life with death; for we are always growing, and dying, and . . ."

". . . ten thousand cocksuckers named 'Bob,' " Dickie thought. "And I'll be damned if I have to explain it. What the *hell*, what in the fucking *hell* do they expect is going to happen to this country?"

". . . of the search for peace," the Minister continued; and cleared his throat and glanced down at his notes.

". . . they foreclose on the fucking store, and what do they get for their money? They get a goddamn hole in the ether, enclosed by *wood*, and filled with various assortment of *shit. That* ain't a store," he thought, and shifted naturally, in his mind, as if to address the banker.

"That's not a *store*, Bob. That is not a *store*. A 'Store' . . ."

In the pulpit the Minister looked up and jiggled his glasses to fix them on his nose. He took the left lens by the frame, with his thumb at the bottom, and his middle finger on top, and jogged the frame once or twice to set it correctly on his nose.

"A *store,* you stupid fucking shit, is what the man who *is* the store has put in to it. Let me ask you something:" In his mind he was behind the counter at the store, and leaning forward, in the attitude of a preceptor, firm in the cause of truth; and the banker, in his mind, sat on the folding chair, by the stove, next to the rack with the auto accessories, from which Dick, in his mind, drew his example.

His simple, open-handed gesture toward the rack invited the banker to turn and look, as Dick's gesture said, at the simple, mundane, and close-to-hand objects in the world, which, nonetheless, to the mind of the educated, contained a lesson.

"Carnauba *wax,*" he said, "what price do you see on it . . . ?"

"Growth and death, of a *farm,*" said the Minister, ". . . of a *tree,* of," here he nodded, as if to say, "Yes, I will allow it, how can I not?" ". . . of marital *love.*

"All things, if we look at them with a respect — and I will not even say 'born of a love of God' — born, let me say, from a confession of our *ignorance,* we see that what passes for knowledge, in our lives — and, listen to me, friends, for I am going to use a word you've heard before, but, I don't think, in this context — what passes for *knowledge* . . ."

Dick had finished making his point to the banker, and he waited, in his fantasy, while the man, abashed, searched for a response.

". . . what we call knowledge is *Idolatry,*" the Minister said, and set his neck, as if he were facing an antagonist, and that antagonist was his assembled congregation.

He looked at them, almost glaring. His eyes moved over the small crowd, which waited, polite, and not uninterested, to hear what he would say next. "I love this sermon," he thought, as he adjusted his glasses.

"I think that it would be possible," he thought, "if I gathered, and *pruned* some writings of mine . . ." In his mind he was assembling them into a small book, and was determined not to think of it as "a book of sermons"; "For who would want to read a book of sermons?" he thought.

Down in the first third of the Church, on the Minister's left, Dick and his wife sat. Dick in a white shirt and a thin, black knit tie.

"My friends," the Minister intoned. Dick's wife reached over to him and took his hand. Dick nodded, to say, "Yes, the simplicity of it moves me, too." He gave her hand a small squeeze, denoting not zeal, but marital togetherness.

The Minister looked quickly down, then snapped his head up and said, "*Idolatry.* Is the feeling that we, in *any* way, are superior to God."

"Then *take* the fucken store," Dick thought. He had gone to the point, as he did each time he played out the fantasy, where he must win the banker's heart. And he found himself unable to imagine how it was accomplished. And, so, as he always did, he skipped past this point and went on.

He had won the banker's heart, convincing him by

reason, appeal, and emotion. The banker sat numb. "But what is the son of a bitch going to do now?" Dick thought. "What can he do now? *Although* I've convinced him? Tear up the *mortgage?* Well, he doesn't have the power. Carry me six more months? If it costs him his job? Bullshit. *Bullshit.* Why am I wasting my time with him? *Fuck* him."

"*Take* the fucking store," he said, and moved into the most satisfying part of his fantasy, in which he opened the cash drawer and emptied it on the floor, then he dug in his pocket and took out a ring of keys. He detached the car keys, and threw the rest onto the pile of receipts. "Fifteen years," he said, and left the man and went upstairs. His wife, at the sink, turned, conscious, somehow, already, of the change, not just in him, but in their future. "Get in the car," he said.

She opened her mouth to speak. "Just get in the car," he said, and walked into his office and shut the door.

There he looked at the mementos fifteen years of his life in the store had brought him. He looked at the deer head, and the calendars, and the framed photos, and the two plaques of appreciation from the high school, and the photograph of him and his wife, dressed as Laurel and Hardy, and he became sad.

". . . and *Godliness,*" the Minister said, ". . . by which, for our purposes, we may mean 'knowledge' . . ." Several members of the congregation nodded. ". . . is reserved for *God,*" he said.

He looked down at the notes, and muttered to himself, as if for emphasis, ". . . reserved for God." His tone softened.

He said, "Let us pray," and there was that soft bustle in the room which Dick always loved.

But that was part of it, too; that he had missed the track. The fellow told him that he'd have to get up early and stay late to get an education. "Yes," Henry thought, "it only accrues when you are not looking at it. Any learning. And how can you *achieve* it, if you're constantly aware of the process? "Yes," he thought, "that must be not part of it, but the sum of it."

He looked at the pebble. It was darker on top, where the deer had dislodged it, coming out of the stream. The others were shades of dull grey to oatmeal white, but this was dark and shiny.

"Battleship Grey," he thought. "This is where he came out. That," he thought, "Is incontrovertible." And he looked at the pebble as a treasure, as it was, for it was his alone, and he felt it to be.

"There is an answer," he thought, "for if the deer went in, he must, then, come out. He must come out *somewhere;* and, and, where he comes out, he must leave a sign." He walked up on the bank.

"There is no god or devil in it."

He began to cast around for the track. As he did so his mind cleared. He was "patterning" the deer; that is, charting its daily movements, over time, to discover its habits. When deer season came he'd use this knowledge to track the deer down, or ambush it, and kill it.

It was three o'clock in the afternoon. He was back in the woods, just up the bank from a stream. The slope continued up through dense, second-growth forest. Pine, mostly, but some maple and birch.

He'd been on the deer's trail for two hours. He had lost it early on, then found it, and followed the tracks down to the stream. He'd cast upstream and down, as the books he'd read told him; first one bank and then the opposite, and had finally located this spot where the deer came out.

He was bent low, walking the edges of a little clearing, looking for the deer's tracks on the carpet of leaves. He straightened up, and realized that he was cold.

Sweat from the walk was cooling on his neck and upper back. He took a deep breath. He reached in the pocket of his wool coat and took out a bandanna and wiped his brow.

He'd loosened his flannel shirt during the two-hour hike. Now he rebuttoned it over the heavy undershirt. He buttoned his coat. "Wish I had worn the vest," he thought.

He shook off the daypack he wore on his back, and set it down on the ground. He took a small deep tin pot from the pack and walked back to the stream and filled the pot with water. He took the pot and a small, flat stone back up the bank.

Back in the clearing he put the pot and the stone down. He scuffed a small patch of ground clean with his boot, and nodded; that's where he would make the fire.

He gathered dead wood in the clearing, and piled it near his water pot. He knelt on the ground and built a little "log cabin" of sticks, about six inches on a side. He put the stone down next to the cabin.

He took some birchbark from the pocket of his coat and tore it into strips, and crumbled the strips into the middle of the log cabin. He looked at the construction for a while, then opened his coat and reached in his shirt pocket and removed a folded piece of eight-by-ten construction paper. He unfolded the paper and tore several long strips lengthwise, and replaced the rest in his shirt pocket.

He took the birchbark out of the middle of the log cabin and laid it to the side. Then put the torn paper where the birchbark had been.

He reached in his pack and took a small, fat white candle from it. He looked at the cabin, and at the bark beside it, and at his small pile of wood.

From his shirt pocket he took a twenty-gauge shotgun shell. Into its empty end was thrust another shell; and the two together made a waterproof match safe. He pulled the shells apart, and took out a blue-headed match and struck it on the seat of his pants. The phosphorus sputtered, but the head flew off. He took another match. He held it with his index finger pressed up tight right beneath the match head, and struck it on his pants. It flamed, and with it he lit the candle, and then the paper in the log cabin. He dropped the match into the flames, and began adding the birchbark.

As the birchbark caught, he dug the candle into the ground, a foot from the fire. He satisfied himself that it would stay upright and burn, then he moved to his pile of wood, and began putting a roof on the cabin — first small twigs, and then some larger ones athwart them.

The fire was catching well. He took some larger

sticks and leaned them over the burning cabin, to form a teepee.

He knelt before the fire, and he thought, as he always did, "This is the origin of prayer"; and it seemed to him magic, for the sun showed that it would be going down, but he'd be warm; and he was thankful.

He reached to the candle, and picked it out of the hole in the earth, and blew it out. He got up stiffly from the ground, and brushed the wet earth from his knees. He felt the candlewick, and found it cool, and dropped it into the neck of the open pack.

"Bishop Berkeley said that the test of truth is: 'Would you trust your life to it?' " he thought. "What is a better test of 'Is it hot?' than 'Can you hold it?' "

"Nothing," he thought.

He stooped for the pot, and, awkward and cold, he upset it. "Well, that's all right, *too,*" he thought.

Back at the stream he filled the pot again, and carried it up the bank. He held it by its thin wire bail, and set it down quickly on the flat rock, which was now inside the fire. He took a tea bag from his shirt pocket and dropped it in the water pot. He stood up and sighed.

At the edge of the clearing was a large, dead log. He pulled it near the fire and sat on it.

"Yes. That was the origin of prayer," he thought. "That's how we learn." The fire crackled and the wind blew in the trees.

"What can approximate it?" he thought. "Why do we try? If I had any courage at all, I'd live out here; and to hell with it. I'd live out here." He closed his eyes and breathed in a bit of the woodsmoke.

"The Indians smoked pounded bark mixed with to-
bacco," he thought; "they could boil water in a
birchbark sack. But they wouldn't heat it. They would
heat the stones, and drop them into the sack; because
there's more than one way to . . ." He opened his eyes,
and saw the water bubbling, and the tea bag dancing in
the pot. He reached a stick and picked the tea bag out,
and dropped it in the fire. He took a metal cup out of his
pack, and pressed it in the ground, to make sure it was
level. He took the stick and levered the bail off the side
of the pot, where it had fallen, and picked the pot up by
the bail. He moved the pot out of the fire, with the stick,
and set it down. He grabbed his bandanna from his
pants pocket, and picked up the bail, and took the pot to
the cup. He used the stick to tip the pot bottom up, and
poured the tea into his cup.

The woods began to go dark in untold shades of
grey. The man sat on the log and sipped his tea.

The teepee had burnt down and fallen in. He re-
plenished the fire, throwing the new thick sticks right
into it.

He held the steaming cup with the bandanna
wrapped around it.

He sat in the woods, and there was no sound except
the crackling of the fire and the wind in the trees.

The man put his hands on her breasts and she arched her
back and was surprised to see him looking at her with
surprise. "Well, isn't this what you wanted?" she
thought. "Oh, hell. If this isn't what you *wanted* . . ."

But then he calmed down and he started moving, and the bed of the truck started to move on its springs.

"Why, he's a heavy one," she thought. "There isn't enough thickness of blanket in the world to keep the ridges of this truckbed off my back," and she thought, "I bet he looks silly," and her mind drifted away, and she looked at the trees and the sky, and at the stars.

"On some of them," she thought, "people are living. That's certain, and I don't care what they say. How can people say they think this or that, when there's *common sense* about a thing, and goddamn those that just don't have it. Goddamn." And she started to list to herself the people she found wanting, the people she hated, who antagonized her through their lack of common sense, or through what she saw as their disapproval of her, ". . . who couldn't last an hour without someone to hold them up, and tell them what to think."

Later, the man wanted to sit in the open door of the truck and talk.

"To what?" she said.

"To sit here," he said.

She looked around. "Why?" she said, and saw that that stopped him.

"A simple word," she thought, ". . . if you can't get beyond *that*. . . . Yes. 'Why?' Like some cigarette ad? And what are you so offended about? Because I wouldn't do something you wanted?"

She looked at him as if sitting in the door, rump perched in the cab, feet on the ground, were the stupidest, most contrived position she could imagine. "You done that before?" she said, and jerked her elbow at him, at his posture. He got up and dusted off the seat of his pants, and looked at her.

"Guess we might as well go back," he said, and she walked around and got in the cab.

Down the highway, alone on the highway, the telephone poles clicked by, off to the side of the wedge of their headlights. The night turned black. "Blacker than velvet," she thought, "blacker-than-velvet," as if the passage of the poles made that sound.

He stopped for coffee. When he cut the lights off, she crunched up her eyes, wishing her night vision to come back quickly, to better appreciate the starry sky when she'd open them. He walked to the doorstep of the diner, and turned back, looking at her. She whisked her finger at the diner door, to say, "Get in, then," and he did.

"Not one of them . . ." she thought. She looked up as she heard the diner's storm door bang shut, and then the closing and the latch of the inner door. A breath of grease and food came out to her, then, in a moment, it was gone, and she craned her neck back and looked up at the sky.

The man ordered two coffees. He turned back on his stool. Out in the parking lot Maris stood, her head thrown back, looking at the stars.

". . . little cunt," he thought.

The counterman asked if he wanted anything else to go with the coffee. He shook his head.

". . . the fuck she playing at?" he thought.

"I'm sorry, mister," the counterman said, "what did you say?"

"*What?*" he said.

"Ast if you wanted anything," the counterman said.

"No. No, I don't," the man said. "I told you that."

The counterman stared at him.

"Something else you wanted to know?" the man said. The counterman looked at him a bit too long for cordiality, then moved away.

Maris came in the door, and the man turned to her. She was stopped by the change in his expression. She looked at him and blinked.

The coffee in the two cups steamed. The diner smelled of cheap disinfectant, and over-used grease.

The man sniffed, and turned back to take his mug of coffee. He looked defiantly down to the counterman, but found him turned away, reading his paper.

He was asleep and his mind was racing; then he was awake and his mind was racing. He tried to remember if thought was always like this. "Yes. No. I don't, how can I remember, when I feel like this?" he thought.

The heating had come on, and he found the sound oppressive. "Why?" he thought; "because of the money? That's not it. What is it?"

The week before he'd taken an aluminum cup from an old, dusty camping outfit on the shelves. He'd used the cup to reheat his coffee through the day, on the pot-bellied stove. And now he remembered stories of kidney patients driven mad.

"And no one knew why," he thought. "And they thought it was despair at the disease, until they discovered that the aluminum reservoir in the machine, what, altered the *water* so that, so that, so, and they were putting *poison* into their . . ."

And it could have been that which, coursing through his body — the coffee, altered by the cup — had caused his mind to race. That he had been contaminated by the metal.

His wife found him in the kitchen, looking through the cupboards over the stove. He turned to her.

"What is it?" she said.

"I didn't want to wake you."

"What is it . . . are you . . . ?"

"I'm fine," he said. She sat down at the table.

"What are you looking for?" she said. He told her about the aluminum. She nodded. He stood there, in his underwear, by the stove, and looked at her. She wore the red plaid bathrobe, and her feet were bare. She looked thin and young. She drew her feet up on a rung of the chair. "Would you like a cup of tea?"

In his mind he saw himself sitting where she sat, and making the tea to comfort him. But it seemed such a world from his place to hers. "Yes. She could come here, or I could go to her, but there is a *world* between what she is, and me."

". . . come on," she said, and got up, and came behind the kitchen island and turned on the stove.

He lumbered by her, and brought a kitchen chair near the window and sat and looked out.

Down on the street he saw the yellow pool of light before the food store.

"No, they always do well," he thought. "*I* don't know. How could they not do well? We have to *eat* . . ."

He knew, as he sat there, that she was not looking at him, and was grateful to her for her respect. "Not that bad. Not too bad," he thought.

The lights went on in the food store.

"Not too bad at all," he thought. "It's the *small* things, that, if there is any meaning in it at *all* . . ."

He heard her pour the hot water in the two mugs. He pressed his face closer to the window. "No, I must concentrate," he thought. "What was it?"

She brought a chair and sat by him. She put the two mugs down on the window ledge and the steam shot up and fogged the cold glass in two mounds.

"Like breasts pulsating," he thought.

"Why do people not kill themselves?"

He felt her arms around him.

She watched the Trooper take his pants, folded so neatly over the back of the chair, and put them on. He smoothed his t-shirt down into the waistband of his pants and sat on the chair to put his boots on.

He looked over at the bed, at her. She smiled at him.

"I don't know," he said. He finished lacing his boots and stood up.

"Why do you always look so *clean?*" she said. "What, is that something you learn in the Service?" He moved into the small motel bathroom, and she heard him washing his hands. She called over the noise of the water: "Is that something you learn in the Service? *Billy?*" He came out drying his hands.

"What is that?" he said.

"To be so *clean* all the time."

"I don't know," he said. She sat on the edge of the bed.

"No shame," he thought. "Buck naked, and it's as natural to her as anything you ever saw."

"You know," he said, "you're a remarkable woman."

"I'm glad you think so."

"Yes. You are," he said.

"God, what is it about her, s'a man never get enough," he thought. "She's so goddamn *natural.*"

She looked up at him. "What? Don't worry, Billy," she said, "what the hell are you *worried* about?"

"Who says I'm worried?" he said.

"Am I going anywhere?" she said. She stood up and walked to the dresser. She bent down and picked her jeans up. She sat on the dresser, put her feet on the cheap, motel chair, and started putting on her pants. "What the hell is the matter, love?" she said. "You know what my number is?"

He walked to the window and looked down at the main street. The movie theater had closed, and the two traffic lights had cycled onto their late-night constant yellow blink.

"All the shops closed," he thought. "Everyone home." One car came through the street, moving too fast, a late model car with a vinyl roof. "Probably out-of-state," he thought, "Probably a salesman." He walked to the bed, and bent down to retrieve the holstered revolver. He clipped the gun and holster inside his belt. She walked to the closet and took down the plaid wool shirt, and brought it to him.

"Anytime you want to call me, you call that number up," she said. He took her and kissed her.

"Well, shit — this fucken nonsense in my head," he thought, "if *it* would go away . . ." And when he sat in the station wagon the thought still persisted.

"She's right. She was *always* right; and if there's two worlds, then the one she lives in is the right one; and what the hell am I torturing myself about, what I want to know . . .

". . . why the hell has every damn thing got to come out even?"

He flicked the lights back on, and drove the last few hundred yards down the blacktop, and up the dirt-road turn-off to his house.

He got out of the car. A cold breeze blew across the yard. He saw the bottoms of the birch leaves twittering in the moonlight, and smiled, thinking, "Well, that's right, *too* . . ."

The breeze died, and he sniffed to the left, then to the right, on his shoulders, to see if he could smell the woman, then he walked to the house.

Nine

The press in the room was almost too great to let him move. He did now, as the men ahead moved, slowly, trying to control his impatience, as they did.

The scoreboard, up at the far wall, read, *Home* and *Visitors*. The baskets, at each end of the room, were canted back up toward the ceiling. The rings and ropes, hooked to the ceiling, were caught and held against the gym's side walls.

The raised stage at the far end was, like the floor, covered with display tables. The men moved from one table to the next, looking down.

" 'Is there some way,' " Henry thought, "that is what they think, 'Is there some way I could move faster than the crowd — If I worked for one of the fellows who has a display . . . ?' or, 'If I had a special *badge* or something . . .' " He moved on shuffling, pushed by the crowd behind him, to the next table. "That is what they'd think," he thought. "But what sort of badge? What sort of badge would that be? A reporter?" he thought, " 'I'm a reporter doing a story,' " he rehearsed to himself.

"Yessir? Help you?" The man behind the table said.

". . . but there's a Providence," Henry thought, "which kept me from proclaiming those things I am not. And I am grateful for it. For that would be the worst lie."

"Help you?"

". . . to claim another man's experience." He looked at the man behind the table. He had black dirty hair going grey. He wore a cardigan over a green flannel shirt. The name tag on the sweater read "Carrolton Arms. Arms for the Hunter and Sportsman. Jack Carrol."

Henry looked at the guns on the table. They were a motley assortment of pistols showing various degrees of neglect. The man behind Henry said, "Mauser. H.S.C.," and Jack Carrol said, "Uh huh." He took a pair of wire-rim reading glasses from the pocket of his shirt, and snapped them open and put them on.

The man nodded, at a point beyond the Mauser.

"Smith, Model 10," he said.

"S'right . . ." the exhibitor said, and nodded, to say, ". . . suit yourself." He picked the revolver up, and gently swung the cylinder out. ". . . s'cuse me," he said to Henry, as he handed the gun to the man behind him.

Henry moved on.

". . . holster wear. Cop's gun," he heard the man say. "Nnn. Ain't been shot much."

Henry moved on. On the next table he saw patches of color. There were books and brochures and advertising items in red and green. A fat man and his wife stood behind the table. The man wore an expensive tweed sport coat. Henry moved on to the table, shielded from the crush for a moment by the man behind him who was discussing the Mauser pistol.

On the new table was a mustard-yellow tin canister marked "Behemoth Powder." The tin bore a rendition of a rampant bear. Around the bear was a red circle, and around the circle, a triangle made up of three muskets.

"Pretty, isn't it?" the man in the sportcoat said.

Henry looked up. "Yes. It is."

"Lost art of lithography," the man said, "pick it up."

Henry picked the tin up. He saw it on his desk, full of pencils of various lengths, the four-inch square tin of Behemoth Powder in soft mustard yellow.

"Brockton Projectile Powders. Company went out of business 1924. Drove out by DuPont. Brockton, Mass. Surprising they held out so long. But, in the period . . . you'll stop me if you know this . . . ?"

". . . no . . ." Henry said.

". . . following the War, they came out with the most magnificent *lithography* . . ."

"The *Bear* for the *Behemoth* line, and the Lion for the *Whitehunter*," the woman said.

"Whitehunter cartridge board, 1910, went, Sotheby's, nineteen *thousand* dollars, Year ago, Spring," the man said.

"That right?" Henry said.

"I hope to tell you," the man said. "You a collector?"

". . . yessir?" the woman said, and Henry turned to

see her talking to the man behind him, who examined the revolver. He now held a small paper bag, stapled with a receipt at the top. He put the bag down heavily on the table.

"You a collector?" the man said to Henry.

"No. I just appreciate good . . ." he said, and looked at the small white tag taped by its string to the bottom of the powder tin.

". . . don't blame you," the man said.

The tag read three hundred twenty dollars.

"You're *interested* in that — a collector — I could do something," the man said. Henry put the tin down. Next to it, on the table, was a display of embroidered cloth patches. He picked up a green and white patch that depicted a fish jumping. It read "Minnesota Fish and Game — 1946."

"How much is this?" Henry said.

"Five bucks," the man said.

The man with the pistol in the paper bag talked to the woman intently. Henry dug in his pocket, and gave the man five dollars, and took the fish patch.

"Let me give you a card," the man said, and put the card and the patch into a small paper bag. He took the bag, not bigger than a postcard, from beneath his table. He popped it open, whipping it through the air, and put the card and the patch into it.

"Thank you," Henry said. He took the bag and folded it, and put it in his shirt pocket, and he was pressed on, down the aisle, by the men behind him.

"I'll put it on my canvas hat," he thought. "I'll put it on my hunting coat. I'll tack it on the wall of my cabin, near my desk. I'll keep it in a drawer of my desk. Wouldn't the tin have looked nice? No doubt it is a good investment. But who's to say? And, after all, you are robbed when you buy it; and, then, again, when you go to sell it. For you're playing the other man's game. Every time. And they make the market. Who's to say it's worth three hundred dollars, or *three* dollars, or *anything?* And, then, why would we want to sell it, if I enjoyed it and kept my pencils in it all those years? Why would I sell it, unless I had fallen on hard times; and, if I had, isn't it always the way that there would be no market for the thing? It *is.* It's an *illusion,*" he thought. "It's an illusion."

He came to the end of the aisle, and crossed the aisle, through the swarm of men, to move back down the other side, down the opposite row of displays, and he sighed. So much to see. So many people, just like him, waiting to see it.

How nice it would be if most of them were gone. He could have talked longer to the man with the powder tin. He could have looked an hour at his other merchandise. A man bumped into him.

"I beg your pardon, sir," Henry said.

"I beg your pardon," the man said.

On the table opposite him were Civil War muskets, laid side-to-side, the muzzles pointing toward the aisle. Two men in battle fatigues leaned over them, talking with the man behind the table. One of the men shook his head and pointed at the musket. The man behind the table smiled, and said something that Henry couldn't hear to the other two men, who laughed. Henry was pressed on by the men behind him, and moved slowly down the aisle.

The Trooper sat in the cruiser and the wet snow came down. "We will be punished for our sins," he thought. "A short blow to the solar plexus, three fingers above the navel, will or should immobilize an assailant, and this blow has the benefit of starting from a seemingly innocuous position.

"Oh, yes," he thought, and remembered the smell of sweat in the gym, and the strange orange-beige tiles, and the feeling there of camaraderie.

"When you are telling a man that on which his life may depend, you don't have to tell him twice," he thought. He remembered the feeling on his hands, and on the back of his neck, from the mat burn in the high-school wrestling room. But at the Academy the mats were old, and not sponge-foam, but canvas-covered, and they puffed dust when a man hit them, and they burned you pretty good, too, when you skidded across them.

The radio cackled. It did not concern him. He cracked his window and lit a cigarette, forbidden in the cruiser. He flipped the match out, and blew smoke out of the window.

"Pain-avoidance inducements," he thought. "Pain-avoidance inducements. And the boxing coach said, 'However big a man is, I'd like to see him bench-press one hundred seventy pounds with his *nose*.' " He smiled.

"That big fat lovely faggot," he thought. "Wouldn't I like to have *him* on my side in a barroom fight. *Lord* that man was big. What *didn't* he know?"

" 'You hook, lads,' he said, 'hook the left foot unobtrusively in the leg of the barstool, and pull it towards you, thrusting the heel of the right hand in the man's face. He's going on his ass.' "

And that worked. And the short jab with the baton, using the short end. " 'Scant six inches from the handle, hold it loose, b'ween the thumb and forefinger, and bring it up smartly, to that point three fingers above the navel. That's where the nerves are centered. How big they are? Don't mean nothing. But how much *heart* does the man have, and What Does He *Know?*' "

" 'Here's a lever you can use, Lever a man right out of his car. Sit down and watch closely, the *added* benefit, correctly executed, you cannot see the baton. N'y'one behind you, and it looks as if the fellow doubles over, leans out of his car, s'is'if he's throwing *up*. Or *praying*. Now don't discount it.' "

And he did it, and it didn't look as if the subject was throwing up. Or praying. But it didn't look as if he were being moved by the baton.

" 'And there's no such *thing* s'a dangerous weapon — I c'd kill you with my belt. It is the *man*.' "

But that look of all-the-nerves-at-once, he'd seen only the one time, and not on a man, and not from the baton. "The look," he thought. "Which, I know what it looks like. Feller at Camp said, you catch 'em there with a slug, and they fold in the middle, pick 'em up, just like y'r hanging bag, y'take to the Airport."

The lights started coming up the hill. He flicked the windshield wipers on. The car was below, coming up the switchback, up to the plain where the cruiser was parked on the straightaway.

He put the cruiser's headlights on, and switched on the Mars light, and called in, "Twenty-seven Alpha, Twenty-seven Alpha, I am 1038, on route Four, request a 1028 on vehicle . . ." and finished with the license number of the car which was coming toward him. He sighed, and got out of the car, the yellow raingear sticking on the seat. He ditched his cigarette, and closed the door, and stood in front of his cruiser, washed in the blue and yellow and red lights.

He maneuvered the butt of his pistol through the slit in his raincoat. He put the hat on, and he shone the flashlight at the car, as it slowed. Back and forth, across its windshield, he played with the flashlight. And moved his right hand, palm flat to the ground, slowly up and down, signaling *stop*.

He stepped to the side of the road, as the oncoming car slowed and stopped, and when he heard the driver put it in Park, he walked up to the driver's side, and tried to look into the car. He made out two people in the front seat. "What's in the back?" he thought. The driver started cranking the window down. The Trooper circled quickly behind the car, and came up on the off side. He strained his eyes, and saw no one in the backseat, no one on the floor.

In the front seat were two women. He tapped on the passenger window and the window came down. "D'you cut off your engine?" he said.

The woman driving looked at him. Obviously frightened. Two women in their early thirties. Short hair, worn down jackets, not well-off, not farm people. Teachers, perhaps; social workers. City people, come up here and been a while.

"What . . . what?" the passenger said.

"Your engine," he said. And the driver cut it off. He shined his Maglight into the backseat. He knew there was no one there, and did it anyway.

"What . . ." the passenger started. He stepped back.

"Sorry to detain you," he said.

". . . what . . . ?"

"Just a check. I'm sorry to have inconvenienced you," he said, and touched the brim of his hat. He stepped just forward of the car, on the right side, and waved his light, to say, "Drive on." He saw the women look at each other. Just the faintest glance, meaning, "OK. Well. We'll discuss it later. At length. Now let's get out of here." And they started the engine. He saw the beginnings of indignation in the passenger. And, as the car went past, he knew that she was looking at him. He felt it, as he looked down, pretending to be occupied with the process of switching off his flashlight. Then they were gone. He walked back to his car.

He whipped the rain from his hat and threw it into the backseat. He tried to whisk some of the water from his coat, and got back in the car, uncomfortable and cold.

He picked up the microphone, and called in, as he lit another cigarette.

"Twenty-seven Alpha is 1024."

He shivered and checked the heater. He found he had one more notch of fan to warm the car with. He turned the fan up and sighed.

He shrugged, as if to say, "Well, then, I'll *do* it"; and worked his way brusquely out of the rain slicker. "No, I don't care if this son of a bitch tears or not," he said; and the slit for his pistol caught on the keys on the Sam Browne belt. He cursed and worked the raincoat free, and balled it and tossed it into the backseat.

"The baton, the mace, the cuffs — best brass knuckles you'll ever find, and *they* will end the argument," the man said, and demonstrated the blow on him. "And the *keys*: look here:" In the cruiser, he repositioned the keys back on his belt.

"Pop the catch, the keystrap, lettem drop into your hand, you catch the loose end of the strap, what have you got? You've *got* a blackjack. You swing *that* over your head, down, down, right side the ear, you're *going* to take out that man's collarbone. Use your whole body. *Swing* that thing. You're down to that for your weapon, lad, *use* it. *Any* of these moves, you get inside that man's defenses — use it *now*. Use it *right* now. You want to use *surprise,* and you do *not* want, be forced, use it twice."

"And, as he always said," the Trooper thought, " 'You follow me?' and grinned."

The Trooper thought back to that grin, and to the man's so obvious love of those in his care, and to the close feeling in the gym, and the surprise and the delight of the women and the men who shared it, and the light down through the slats, slanting over the floor, the way it looked in the mornings, and the way it looked in the afternoon; and the woman at home who looked like she had been struck three fingers above the navel, when she'd found out about the girl in town.

When Henry drove up to the store the snow was stopping. He pulled the car to the gas pumps. He looked at the store, and saw Dick behind the counter. Dick rose at the sound of the car pulling up, then saw that it was Henry. Henry waved, and Dick nodded, and settled back on his stool.

Henry gassed the car, then backed it away from the pumps and walked into the store. He knocked the snow from his boots.

" 'leven-twenty," Henry said. Dick looked up slowly.

" 'leven-twenty."

"Set it down?" Dick said.

"F'you would," Henry said. Dick took Henry's receipt pad from the shelf and wrote the number in it. Henry walked down the aisle.

"Thread," Henry said.

"Thread, yes. Kind of thread?"

"Sewing," Henry said. "N'y *other* kind of thread?" he said, with a light smile on his face. There was a pause.

"Trussing a *turkey*," Dick said. Henry turned and looked at Dick.

". . . and other kinds, too. I'm sure."

"Trussing a turkey. Yes. that's true," Henry said.

Dick cleared his throat, and put his head down, and pretended to write on the notepad.

The snow was falling around the car as Henry drove home, and he pictured the various postures he could adopt in the hunting jacket, and the placement of the fishing patch on it. "I think I could put it on the high left side," he thought, "above the existing pocket." He saw himself in the woods in the jacket, turning, as to some sound, as to some sense not yet a sound.

He reached in his shirt pocket and took out the small paper bag and ripped open the top, where the man had stapled it. He felt for the stiff patch; and, driving with his left hand, he held the patch with his right pressed against his upper chest on the left side, just beneath the collarbone. He steered the car with his knee, and took his left hand to the rearview mirror, and tilted it. In it he saw the patch held against his jacket, as it would look when it was sewn. He smiled at the patch — the fish, accidentally, providentially, having occurred in the correct, upright position as he took it from the bag.

He would sew it on his jacket. He would stitch a small round compass beneath it, so he would always have it with him in the woods. The jacket smelled damp, and he shook his head over it. To have it dry-cleaned would take some of the life out of the wool, no matter what they said. "Which is a good example," he thought, "of trusting your *senses,* rather than listening to things *people say. What wouldn't* they tell you . . . ?"

*   *   *

He sat at the kitchen table, with the jacket on his knees. He found some crumpled birchbark in one pocket, and an old shopping list, half-torn. He had used the other half for what? And twigs, and the brass shell of a .308 cartridge, and he put them on the kitchen counter, near the sink. He looked at the place where the patch would be. "What does it mean?" he thought, "*any* case? To 'have' something? What in the hell does it mean? And if we have one, we want more, and then we can't sleep. If I hang the coat *up*," he thought, "and let it rain, and let the wind blow on it, that would take the smell out, but she . . ." He looked around, as if she could hear him thinking, convinced that she could. "Isn't that funny?" he thought. "A rational man, if I tried to *explain* it . . ." He pulled himself backwards, up, till he was sitting on the counter, with the coat across his lap, his hands resting upon it lightly, as if it were a stadium blanket, and he sat very still.

Marty was in the woods, and wearing the green army jacket. He had promised his wife he would wear the blaze orange safety vest over it, but he'd never had the slightest intention of doing so. And he was silent in the woods, as he always was, and never made an unnecessary sound, or spoke a word at all if he could help it; and many times, with an unschooled companion, or his wife, on the few outings they made together, or his son, when they would speak, he'd raise his finger to his lips, not unkindly, but direct, to quiet them.

For you had to be like it if you wanted to be part of it.

His father had told him, when he was ten, ten or twelve, that if you came into your house, the moment you came in, you'd know if there was a deer in there or not. And Marty thought that that was evident, and foolish, when his father had said that. "Well, out here, you're in the *deer's* house," his father said.

"And we should *never* underestimate *any* opponent," Marty thought, "or wish for them to be stupid, or badly prepared, or undergeneraled; but always be *assured* that they are *as* brave, *as* prepared, *as* unconventional, *as* smart, and by-damn as lucky as *we* are; and then go out there and just think that much harder."

And he'd been out there, his back against the tree, since before dawn, and he was satisfied that he'd moved in nicely, and settled in nicely, and quit, the wind in his face, his field of vision good, down the slope, to the bank of the stream, where he commanded a field of view some hundred yards to either side, down the stream, and, across the bank, back into the thick woods.

He'd sat there while the sun came up, and had seen the time before the false dawn, when there was, more than light, a feeling in the air of change, when the air became, as he put it, rough-looking, and then it started to get light, and then it got light.

Through the morning, he resisted the urge to check his watch, to drink, to sleep, to move, to urinate. "I can sit here for days, I can sit here forever," he thought. The rifle was comfortable across his legs, his back was comfortable, against the large maple. He'd sat there for hours, his breathing slowed, gradually becoming part of the forest. He'd seen the chimpmunk, hours ago, and watched it with the barest movement of his eyes, not moving his head, as it ran up the tree, limb to limb, and back again, and then down the trunk, and up the streambed, out of his vision.

And he knew when it was about ten o'clock, and possible that the deer would come down to drink; and when it was around two o'clock, when it was also possible that they'd be moving. But nothing had moved, through the day, but the chipmunk.

He'd heard the one plane, far overhead, at midday, flying to Labrador, he thought, or Iceland, or over the pole, and he'd not looked up. "It was a white line in the sky," he thought, "a chalk line up in the sky, and I heard it, and I know what it means, and there's no reason for me to look at it."

Through the day, he'd seen the broken branch on the stump on the far bank, and thought, fifty times, a hundred times, "It's a deer bedding," and adjusted his focus, and seen it for what it was. And, later, hours on, he'd see it again, and think, "Yes it was that branch that once, but now it might be . . ." Then he would observe it, until he was, again, satisfied it was what it was; and an hour would pass, and the light would change, altering everything, and the slow sweeps of his eyes would once again take in the branch, and he would say, "That's in the place where, earlier, I saw the branch, but now, odd as it is, I swear that it looks to me as if . . ." And it was at one of the moments when he was looking at the branch, that he heard the twig snap. He was completely alert, and had unconsciously moved his finger the merest fraction to click off the rifle's safety, when he heard another twig snap, then a third, and he was angry, for he knew it could be nothing other than a man.

He saw Henry moving heavily down to the streambed. He saw the flash of an embroidered patch high on his jacket, and something white, just inside the open coat, at his belt, and saw it was the ivory stocks of a revolver. Henry moved over the stones in the stream, holding his rifle high, and sweeping the banks with his eyes.

He swept his glance right over Marty, who knew he would not be observed, then moved on. He rounded the bend in the stream, and was gone. Marty waited patiently for the stray sounds of Henry's progress, but no more came.

"Just like the plane," he thought. "It's here, and then it's gone, and whatever you're looking at, is — while it's there — then it passes on."

He lulled himself. "It passes on. And I haven't moved."

He thought about his childhood. He thought about hunting with his grandfather, who told him at one time there had been six hundred men on the mountain, every day, quarrying granite. Who told him they'd go courting, by sleigh, in the wintertime, and the horse and a sleighbell, fixed right up, under the bridle; and when they'd go courting they'd take and pack snow up into the bell, so the girls' parents wouldn't know what time they'd brought her home. He thought about his father's friends, and the things that they told him they'd seen back in the woods. He thought about his time in the Service, and, for longer periods, as the day went on, he thought about nothing, and missed nothing that went on before him and around him.

Then the sun started down, and he found himself getting cold. "But not now," he thought, "no way you're going to move *now,*" and the sun went down, first lingering on, till you thought it would be that blue grey, then that grey, then that white grey forever, then getting dark in earnest, then it was in that period where you said that there was nothing to see in the dark; and then he said it was time to go, as it was so dark there was nothing to be seen, and then, he said, just a few more minutes, as it was impossible that he'd sit all day, so perfectly, and see nothing. And so he sat.

There was no glow from the sky, and no light left in the woods at all when the four deer came down the bank. He made out the buck's horns. "Well, all I have done is wait for you," he thought, "but I have waited for you." As the doe's hooves clattered a stone in the stream he raised his rifle, to see if the scope could catch enough of whatever light there might be, to allow a shot. He saw the buck through his scope, and picked his spot on the buck's shoulder.

Ten

The first time that he'd heard it he didn't know what it was. He thought back to that time, those years ago, and was it a cannon? He had never heard a cannon, but he sensed that that was not what he'd heard, and it was not a gunshot, though it could have been, he thought, to someone who had never heard a gunshot, it was that sharp. Like a whip, he thought, the world's biggest bullwhip. And he remembered how he'd stopped, deep in the woods, and waited, and heard it again.

It was the trees popping in the cold. "Like something wrenched from your soul," he thought, and smiled. "Just like it was torn out of there. And you were free."

He pushed on through the snow. "Uphill or downhill," he thought. "It doesn't matter, the skis do the work." He smiled at his false humility. "No, I'm doing the work," he thought. "Especially uphill. Who else would do it but me? There's no one here but me. My wife is not here. Nothing in my life is here except me. In the woods. A Man in the woods. And if I'm strong enough to navigate in this snow, then I am. And there's no further analysis you need.

"Quite simple," he thought.

He had been following a deertrack through the deep snow, back in the woods. "Blow-down I couldn't get *over* in the Spring — I glide over it," he thought. "Everything changes."

He saw a tree up ahead, and debated, whether to take it on the right or left. The left had thicker brush, and the right was somewhat steeper. As he came up to it, he saw that the deer had hesitated, too. Her tracks started to the right, and then veered left through the brush. He smiled.

"Well, I guess that we all got the same problem," he thought. "And if you're taking your time, you've got the luxury of thought." He moved into the brush, going slowly, one ski, then the other, bending low sometimes. "F'th'deer can do it, so can I," he thought.

Then he was through the brush, and it was a fairly clear run through a clearing, uphill for fifty or so yards. And the sun was making the shadows blue.

"I could stop," he thought. "Hell, I could stop and make tea." His body felt warm, and good, powerful, all buttocks and shoulders. "Warm, now," he thought, and looked up the hill, and pushed off on his skis. They stuck a bit in the snow, as the wax was beginning to wear off. "No wonder, the trash that I've had them over today," he thought. "No wonder at all. You can't ask equipment to do more than's in its nature." As he pushed up the hill, not gliding now, but using the poles, working with his arms. "And the most useless tool," he thought, "is an all-purpose tool. There's no such thing."

He continued up the hill, and found himself getting winded. "No point to stop *here*," he thought, "you have to go in natural *stages*. And the natural *stage*, if you want to stop, is up top, at the top of the clearing." The snow was beginning again. He adjusted his belt, and pulled his pants up. He took the red bandanna from his back pocket, and mopped his brow and neck. "Always the same," he thought. "You go out, and *however* much you know that you aren't going to need it, you always dress too warm." He tied the sleeves of his hunting jacket tighter around his middle, and pushed off, up the hill. "I should have left it on a branch, I went in the woods," he thought. "Pick it up on the way home."

"Aren't humans funny?" he thought. "Make the same mistake once, twice, *every time* in our lives, we are faced with the same dilemma. And then we make up *rules,* about how, when faced with certain circumstances, we should act a certain way. And then, those circumstances *arise,* we find that reason why the rules . . ."

He got to the top of the rise, the top of the clearing, and stood panting. He maneuvered in a circle, to bring himself around, and look back the way he had come.

". . . why the rules don't apply," he thought. He mopped his face and neck again. His arms and back were drenched in sweat, and he found himself getting cold.

"Of course it's cold," he thought. "The sun is going down, and I've been working. People in town. Wonder why they're out of shape. There is a *use* for everything, and *our* use ..."

"And the knife, too," he thought. "No all-purpose tool, no extra-sharp knife 'never needs sharpening.' What is that but idolatry?" And another part of his brain said, "Get home," and he turned his skis, again in the half-circle, and said to himself, "I am not frightened. Why should I be frightened?"

The deertrack veered to his left, back deeper through the woods. "Well, that's fine," he thought. "And I was following you a while, because I *chose* to. And if I choose *differently* ...

"That is the problem," he thought. "No, no. That's the problem. Situations *change* ... isn't that just what I ..."

"You have to go home," the voice said. "Well, there's no shame in *that*," he thought, "I'm *cold*. I'm cold, for godssake, why shouldn't I be? Hard as I've been working, and the sun ..." He looked back over his shoulder, as the woods before him had gone quickly dark. He couldn't see the sun above the trees.

"It doesn't matter if I *can*," he thought, "I'm going *home*. And Home is just to my right," He thought. "Just on my right hand," he found the words comforting and old-fashioned. "Well, that's where it is," he thought. And the North Road is North-northeast, no better than a half-a-mile, wherever I am in these woods. North-northeast, and I have to hit it. Hell, f'I *didn't* have a compass I could wait till night and see the dipper, pick out the polestar, and walk straight North. Whatever is there to it? Nothing to it. Hell, I could follow my *tracks* back," he thought, "*though* it's going dark. And *though* the snow.... F'a man, in the war, or however," he thought. He untied his hunting coat and pulled it on. It didn't make him warm. He buttoned it to the neck and clapped his arms against his body several times, and he felt no warmer.

"Then I'd better get home," he thought. He turned, away from the path the deer took, and pushed off into the woods. There was a thicket before him. "Well," he thought, "if a man did not have an *objective*." He went into it, some vines whipping his face. "But I *do*," he thought, "which is *to get home,* which is only common sense, for the Lord's sake." The jacket hindered him, and his belt felt heavy. He pushed through the thicket.

"Well, fine," he thought. "Well, fine." He came out and found himself in deep woods that he did not recognize.

"It makes no difference," he thought, and thought, at the same time, "Woods are woods," and "I have never seen this land before."

There was a small deer run or path through the woods down and to his left.

"My way is straight ahead," he thought, "but if I can make better time down the hill, I should do it, and correct afterward. Down the hill is East," he thought. "East. And even *East,* I'm getting back to the road. Certainly." He bit his right glove to get it off, and it came off his hand, lodged in the strap of the ski pole. He let the pole and glove drop to the snow and dug in his pants pocket for the compass.

"Down the hill," he thought, and looked up at the

small path, which was darker now, and difficult to distinguish. "Down the hill. East. Ninety degrees." He took the compass in his palm, and held it, waiting for the needle to steady. "Come on," he thought. And looked down at it. "Yes. I'm suppose to put it down, somewhere *flat*. Where could I put it down?" he thought. "You tell *me*. You tell me. What the *hell*," he thought, looking wide-eyed at the compass. And then he thought that it wouldn't steady, as he was holding it too close to metal. "What metal?" he thought, then remembered the gun on his belt, and held the compass out at half-arm's-length. "And then how can I *see* it?" he thought. "But where should I put it *down* . . . ?" He stuck it back in his pocket, and stopped to pick up the ski pole and glove. He tried, awkwardly, to get his hand into the glove, and was hindered by the strap. "I've done this hundreds of times," he thought. "But if there is some reason that I cannot get my hand into the glove while it is in the strap, then . . ." He tried to work the glove out of the strap, holding the ski pole in his hand, and pulling the glove with his teeth.

"This is . . . this is . . ." he thought. He looked back at the woods behind him, which looked black.

"Well, no. I'm going *home*," he thought, and picked up the glove and tried to jam his hand through the strap, twisted in the fabric, and threw it down on the snow, and shot his hand into his pocket for the compass, and he couldn't find it there.

"No. It *is* there," he thought. "It may be that I cannot *find*, I cannot *find* it. But it *is* there, because it *was* there, and it must *be* there, or . . ." He looked down, and saw nothing on the snow except his ski pole and glove. He picked them up. "I will circle *as slowly as necessary,*" he thought, "then I *must* see the . . ." He began to make a circle in the snow. "I must see the compass," he thought.

He made his circle, and didn't see the compass.

"It doesn't matter," he thought, "because I . . ." He looked up, at the end of his circle, and recognized nothing.

"This is ridiculous," he thought. He moved to his right, and then to his left, and recognized, at no point, anything he had ever seen before. He started to cough, and felt cold. "No, I have matches, and I, even if I didn't. I have my gun, and could open a cartridge case, and pour powder on paper, and fire another cartridge *into* it to ignite . . ." As he thought, he hunted in his pocket, and found, by touch, bills, and coins, and a folded book of checks, and, below it, the compass.

He took a deep breath. He took the compass, and held it in his hand. "I am so steady," he thought. He maneuvered, on his skis. "There always is a feeling," he thought, "and I feel that," he looked around, "*this* is North." He looked down at the compass needle, which was swinging between East and West, between Northeast and Northwest, and which was slowly moving in smaller arcs to indicate North was behind him, exactly in opposition to his intuition.

"No," he said. "No, no. That's impossible. I could be *slightly* off, but . . ." He remembered the other compass, sewn underneath the fish patch on his jacket. "Well, *fine,*" he thought, "what is the point of having spares, or having thought ahead to have spares, if you cannot use them in situations just like . . ." He started to put his compass back in the pocket of his pants, then stopped.

"No. No," he thought. "I lost you *once* in there, I will be damned if I . . . I *know* which way is home . . ."

He felt the cold from the snow seeping through his socks and making his feet cold. He reached down and picked up the ski pole. He put his hand through the strap, so it was bunched up with the glove, stuck in there. But he could not grasp the ski pole while holding the compass. He took his cap off his head, and put the compass in it, and put it back on his head. He looked around the woods, to the left and to the right. He pushed off on his skis.

He came to a low place and found his right ski tangled in vines. He tried to wrench it loose, and could not, and backed it out. He crouched low to work himself through the overhanging vines, and pushed himself forward on his hands. Low branches whipped his eyes. He pushed through, and found himself on a bank, gliding, and then falling down.

It was dark, and he was wet, and he was cold.

"I have my gun," he thought. "I can fire for help. Any time. If they were looking for me. Three shots." He reached in his pocket for his compass, then he felt on his head, and found his hat gone.

He got to his feet. He began to tear at the patch on the hunting coat, to get to the compass underneath. He found his ears and his hand beginning to tingle with the early burn of frostbite.

He shook off the ski pole from his right hand, and

tried to open the buttons on his hunting coat. He found he could not do so, and wrenched the coat up to feel for the belt knife on the sheath in back. He found the clasp, and worked to get the knife out, but the heavy coat, bunched at his back, made it impossible. He levered the sheath down, parallel to his belt, and tore the knife out of it, feeling it cut the coat as it came.

He bit his left glove off, and tossed it and the ski pole down. He put the knife handle in his teeth and rubbed his hands together to warm them. He looked down, and, like a surgeon, concentrating so the stitches stood out like cords, he cut the patch from the jacket, and the little cheap red compass fell in the snow. He flung the knife away from him, and sank to his knees in the dark, but he could not see the compass. He dug in the snow with his hands till they were too cold to feel, then he stood and started forward. He stopped, and knelt. He beat his hands against each other, and on his thighs, till he had some feeling, then he worked the release, and stood, and shook his skis off.

He lurched forward through the snow, and found himself stuck, up to his knees.

"No, no. It's not all that deep," he thought, "just here." He trudged, picking his legs up, and moving forward quickly, fitfully, away from the bank, deeper into the woods.

The snow, except where it drifted, was only calf-deep, and he moved through the woods. He came across his ski trail, and looked at it with the half-animal thought it was tainted. He moved on, his breath coming quickly, in pants.

In the dark he fell into the small logging clearing, and saw the ruts of the logging truck, now filled with snow. He followed them, half at a run. He stuck his hands into his pants pockets for warmth, and ran unbalanced. He fell, and levered himself up, onto his knees, and up on his feet, and on. And there was a place where he met another logging road.

"No," he thought. "Well. One way must lead to the North Road." He turned to the left and ran, stumbling down the road for fifty yards, then turned and ran back, past the road he'd come out on. "That is still there," he thought, and ran on, determined to run till he died, and found himself, in twenty seconds, out on the North Road. The sides were plowed and the snow banked up high, the road was gritty with the salt and dirt spread by the Town, and it was punctuated by the regular herringbone of the chains on the tires of the snowplow.

"I'm above it," he thought. "My house is down there." He turned to his right. "I was so *close* to it."

He felt his whole face burning with the cold, and his legs felt like sticks. He had no feeling in his hands. He walked on, and, in a while, came over the hill.

Down below, far below, he saw the bend; and below the bend he saw his house, and the yellow light in the kitchen, and the shadow which was his wife, moving down there, cooking and talking on the telephone.

Eleven

Carl and Marty stood just outside of the garage door. It was a bright day, Carl lifted his head and squinted.

Marty looked across the street, at the three people at the entrance of the hardware store. If they had glanced at him they would have seen him quiet and calm. And, although not impertinent, he would not have acknowledged their gaze.

The one man, at the hardware store, wore a blue suit, and he talked to the man and woman, hands held at waist-level, gesturing gently. Carl looked down, and across the street. "Whallp . . ." he said. Marty shrugged.

When Henry came down the hill he was saying to himself, "Celery seed. Washer for the hose. Mail."

There was a letter in the pocket of his shirt, a legal envelope, crisp and stiff. When he turned his head toward the left it dug into his chin. "There is no way I can forget it," he thought. "All those times," he shook his head, "I am a mystery to myself. 'Don't forget the letter,' 'Do not forget to mail the letter,' 'Put the letter on the seat of the *car*,' and, there I'm driving back up the hill, everything done, and the *letter* still in my pocket. What *is* there, in human *nature* — well, well, well, no. No." He thought, "If, no. No machine was built to fail. Each was designed to, and if we ask: 'What is it I *gain*, through . . .' " Then he saw the cat in the road, like a housecat, but out-of-scale. "Gain through forgetting to mail the . . ." he thought, and looked again, to see it dart across the road, looking like it took up the whole road, one side to the other, a tawny blur of interminable length.

The car was stopped. He sat there with his foot on the brake. His mouth was slightly open. He was looking at the spot where he had seen the cat. For a while he had no thoughts at all, like a man for the brief while after great danger, or orgasm; a relief, rather than a feeling of relief.

"Down at the store they will say," he thought, then lapsed into that calm for a moment again. As he came out of it he cursed himself for his lack of ability to live, as he phrased it to himself, "in a pure state"; and, as he cursed himself, another part of his mind was forming the story he would tell down at the store. The story took form as the impression of the cat receded; and the story started to become the memory, much as the photograph supplants and reduces the unnamed feeling of the moment it records.

"You fool," he thought; and, at the same time, " 'Wal, guess what I saw today.' Or, 'Saw an interesting

thing, com'n down the hill.' Or, 'You know, I'd been
told they were *extinct,* and I'd believe it, save that . . .' "
    "Or, 'One could,' " though he knew he would not do
it, and debated for an instant if he'd refrain from a good
dramatic sense, or from a lack of self-control. "One
could say 'Celery seeds . . . ?' and Dick would say,
'How's *Henry* today . . . ?' and all that, and, checking
out, he'd say, 'Set it down . . . ?' and I'd say, 'Dick . . .
Dick: I saw a mountain lion today.' 'The hell you say!'
so on. I could shrug, I don't know what I'd do, then lean
on the counter and tell him. Next man would come in,
Dick would say 'Henry, Henry, *tell* 'im . . . ,' and I'd
back off, just a bit, and he'd insist, of course, he'd be
saying, how could I *not* tell him what I'd seen. Various
things they'd say. That they thought they were *extinct,*
or So-and-So's *mother* said she saw one, way back. Before the War, but the Fish and Game came out, and *told*
her that they were extinct . . ." He shook his head, and
smiled, with that private knowledge of those who have
been there. "And I remember *hearing* that, too," he
thought. "That someone was, not 'scorned,' but . . . not
'*scorned,*' but . . ." He caught the car out of the corner
of his eye, in the rearview mirror. He wondered how
long it was sitting there behind him; and the exhaust, for
the instant, seemed to him like steam, of a fuming crea-
ture, angry at him. He moved his car over to the right,
and waved the car past. It came past slowly, and he
waved at the driver, a woman from Town, he knew to
say hello to. She did not wave back.
    "And it's good that she came," he thought, as I
would have *forgotten* . . ." Two parts of his mind spoke,

one defending, which said, "No, you wouldn't," and the other, "Yes. You would, you know how you are," to which he responded, "I'm up, near the ravine, just above the spot where I always see the doe, below the turn, just below Williams," speaking, irritated, to that portion of his mind. "And the *tracks* are there, *any* case. How could they *not* be?"

He started the car up, angry, and drove, slowly, as if to impress himself with his rectitude. "Altogether too much is *made*," he thought, "of . . . and the *hell* of it, is, I saw a mountain lion. If they say they're extinct, or not, that's all the better. I don't *give* a damn. And if twenty men working for a month could not find a track, *well*. And if they said that I was *crazy* . . ." He paused. "*But*," he thought, "if it fell out, like that Old Woman, who they said, 'Twn'y *years* ago, old So-and-So,' and, of course, I'd be old then, or dead. Who is to say I am not old now? '. . . *they* saw a . . . fellow lived at the old Bailey place, said he saw a moun'lion. Fish and Game came in and . . .' If I was the person in that story . . ." he thought. Well, well, *all right,* now. And, perhaps, I'm being punished, for not recognizing how that Old Woman felt. For there *was* a story, and I *heard* it, and I'm sure there *was* an Old Woman," and then a different thought came in, and it said, "Though, I am not sure she saw a mountain lion. What was to stop her," he thought, "from saying any damn thing that she chose?" He rounded the curve, just below the Village, driving slowly.

"And is it not," he thought, "a process of con-

sensus?" He gestured, as if to an opponent, saying, "There's the simple fact."

"Consensus," he thought. "The *Community* — for what is 'law'? — decided what it *means*, and who is *guilty*, and who . . ." He slowed down.

"Like the *oaths*. Medieval times. Where they had Trial-by-Oath. They would take, if you asserted something, you could bring in twenty friends, and if they *swore*" — he made a gesture of acknowledgment — "according to a formula — if they *swore*, that you were an honorable . . . 'man,' or, what, or 'businessman,' then you'd prevail. But if one *faltered*, or *altered* a syllable of the oath . . ." He shrugged, meaning, "What could you do . . . ?"

"But *then*:" he thought, and smiled, "the *beauty*, which no one has *mentioned*, though *I know* this was the essence of the exercise, is that you had to have twenty friends, loved you enough to come into Court; and who you *trusted*, believe in you *that extent* they wu'nt be flustered, and . . .

"Aha," he thought, "did not have a *grudge* against you, sufficient, they'd 'accidentally' let a syllable slip. And the *true* beauty . . ." He pulled over the bridge, and looked at the house, by the bridge. "It looks dark," he thought, "but always looks dark. I don't know if they've moved away, or . . ."

A truck passed, on the blacktop, and he waited for it to pass and then pulled out over the bridge, and took a left on the blacktop.

"Isn't that odd . . . ?" he thought. "We say, 'So many

mysteries,' but *all* of it, if you think about it. And I'm *sure* . . ." He parked, across from the hardware store. "I'm sure there were *countless* instances, they took the Oath, where a witness would stumble, and the Judge, *speaking for all the people,* would say that it was allowed, and it didn't hurt the defendant's case, and, all the people agreed, because they said 'Well, we know So-and-So has a *stutter,*' or 'They have been *ill,*' or 'no, we mis-*heard* them,' and that there were *rules,* which allowed the Judge, or the Community — for what, of these things, are ever tried, except in the mind of the community — ?" he thought, pleased with himself. He got out of the car, and started to stroll across the street. "Because it is the *Community* which . . ." He walked toward the store, and, as he walked, he slowed. And he stopped, on the sidewalk, and looked at the padlock on the door.

The Trooper had been on a call on the interstate, and followed the bodies down to the hospital. He sat in the waiting area, finishing his report. It was past the end of his shift, and he was tired. The sun was long up, and he was hot in his uniform. It felt stiff with sweat and dirt. He wanted to go home.

"Fellow in Germany, the News, they did this report on the speed limits," the Doctor said. "No speed limits. The Autobahn. Mercedes, whatever, do a hundred fifty miles an hour. The report, 'Do you have more accidents here,' the speed limits. Fellow says, 'we do not have more accidents, but those we *do* have are more spectacular.' "

The Doctor sat down on the vinyl chair, and drank his cup of coffee. But the Trooper was tired, and didn't want to chat. He sighed. "I'm going home," he said.

"Goin' home, Bill?" the Doctor said.

"Yeaauh," he said, breathing it out, like the last breath of something pneumatic. He stood.

In the cruiser he got the call, and the call took him to the Quarry.

Afterwards, coming down the hill, he wished he could go home and change, shower, and have a cup of coffee, as if that would make it better. And he wished that someone would have preceded him to Marty's house, and it seemed likely that that would be so. But when he pulled up, he saw the shades quickly drawn back, and he knew that he was the first. "Well," he thought. "That's right. That's my job."

He got slowly out of the cruiser, not, now, from reluctance, but from respect. And as he closed the door, he heard the porch door of Marty's house open, and he looked up.

Marty had come three steps out of his house onto the porch.

In the living room the Trooper saw his family, and also the girl's mother sitting, as they'd been sitting all night, and there was Marty, out on the porch. The Trooper started to raise the hand that held his hat, and he stopped, halfway through the gesture, and laid it on the roof of the car, and came around the car. As he did so, Marty came down the steps. The Trooper, seeing him, stopped at the sidewalk, and Marty came down to him.

Marty stepped down the sidewalk, and the Trooper stepped with him, one step, two steps, almost like young people at the end of a date, several steps down the sidewalk, and they stopped.

". . . both of 'em?" Marty said.

"The girl's going to the Hospital. It don't look good," the Trooper said. "Your boy's dead." He paused. "Both of 'em, a fall, up the Quarry."

"Waaaal, I knew it, th'other kids came back. Last night," Marty said. He nodded his thanks at the Trooper, and started to turn, back toward the house. ". . . *Bill*," he said.

"I'd like. To come in. To pay my Respects. To Marge," the Trooper said. Marty turned back. With that look that only comes with death. "No. You're right," the Trooper said. They stood there a moment. "I'm so sorry, Mart."

"What are you, going home now?" Marty said.

"No. I've got to tell the girl's parents."

". . . the mother's in there." He shrugged toward his house.

"I saw her in there," the Trooper said.

"Ed's home, by the phone. Well," he said briskly. "Th'ain'no more put'n it off," and smiled, and turned and walked back to his house.

"But I can't tell you," Mrs. Bell said. "The times I have said to *confine* them, or, I don't know, just put them on some *retreat* . . ." Rose turned back from sorting the mail.

"What would that be?" she said.

"What? Well, a *resort*. Lord knows, they're *empty,* Spring. Get a, well, look: get a group. Now. Th'French Canadians. Go down. They go to Florida, or come here, the *leaves* . . . ?" Rose nodded.

"All right. You shop, travel agencies, State Chamber of *Commerce,* n'you get a special group *discount,* take ovr'a a, all right, I hate to say it, a 'motel,' a *ski* resort, it doesn't have to be a motel. But it's a crime, let them, what do they do, drink and drive, drink and drive, drink and *drive,* and go *kill* themselves, and I'm sorry. They want to have sex? What is to *prevent* them" — she stopped herself — "I'm not saying 'give them *rooms*' . . ."

"What?" Rose said.

"I said that I'm not suggesting we give them *rooms* at the resort."

"All right," Rose said, and smiled.

"No, Rose. I'm not saying that, and you know that I'm not. What I am *saying,* and you watch, if this is, ten, fifteen years, if you don't see this is what the majority of school districts, the State, come to. And I'll tell you why, because we cannot live, with the alternative. I swear to God. Every year. Every year." She shook her head, and then she stopped speaking, and Rose turned around to see her friend, head down, sobbing. She walked over to the counter, and stood by her.

Twelve

Out by what had been the woodpile he saw the lost wedge, the glints of sliver where the maul had battered it, and the remnants of the old green paint. "Never'd of seen it, the old, wet chips," Henry thought. He picked it up, and rubbed the surface dirt off on his old wool pants.

"Take it up, take some steel wool to it, brighten it up, *paint* it. . . . I hate, put some *Day*-Glo, something on it," he thought, that's the way to *keep* 'em, certainly, but." He shook his head, thinking, "It just goes against my grain."

He walked, over the carpet of the sodden chips, to the garden, and opened the gate. "I don't know why," he thought. "Deer jump a six-foot fence, and they could go over this easily, but they never come in here." He shrugged and walked toward one of the beds. The wind blew one puff of cool air up from the pond. He looked down. "*Oh* yes," he thought. "*There* you are." He squatted and dug around the wilted, green shoot of leaves, till he bared the top of the carrot. "Just as good as last year," he thought. "Better." He dug his fingers down to get a grip, and worked the carrot loose. He stripped the dirt off, and wiped his hands on his pants. The carrot was still streaked here and there with red-brown earth. ". . . never hurt anyone," he thought.

He bit the top off, and spit it away.

He turned back toward his house. Inside the garden, he juggled the wedge and the carrot; and ended, with the carrot in his mouth, and the wedge under his arm, pressed to his side, as he opened the gate.

After he passed through, he affixed the loop of wire which held the gate closed. He walked toward his house, thinking of paint for the wedge, and settled on yellow; "An old-time yellow," he thought.

In his mind, he saw himself, driving down this afternoon, to the store, to buy the paint. Then, he remembered that the store was closed.

"Well, then, I'll drive down to Town," he thought, and planned that trip in his mind.

Down the road they came, and around the bend, up the small rise, and onto the flat. A pickup, coming down the other way, slowed and stopped, respectfully, until he realized that to wait he would likely be stuck there for half an hour.

He caught Marty's attention, and Marty moved the group onto the shoulder. The driver touched his forefinger to the brim of his cap; then moved the truck, oh so slowly, past them, and, even having passed them, continued slow down the road, past the point where there was the least chance the group might look and see him.

Two men raised the white bar, and the group formed, in the cemetery, in three ranks.

On a command, the color guard came forward — four men, the two outermost with M-1 Carbines, the two in the middle each with a flag. They halted, and, on command, came to Parade Rest.

The State Flag dipped. The American Flag was held high, and popped once in the breeze.

Lynn saw them in the cemetery, and realized he had gotten the time wrong. He'd taken the time they expected to be at the cemetery for the time of their assembly in the Town, and had allowed the extra forty minutes for their parade up the hill. He had counted on being early, and looked forward to the solitude; but now, here they were, and already assembled, and he thought that this was not inferior to his plan. He came down the road slowly, and stood outside the white rail fence, removed his hat, and listened to the speech.

"... Korea, Bataan, Leyte, Sicily, Normandie, Belgium ..." The Minister paused ever-so briefly, "Vietnam," he said, inclining his head, not in anyone's particular direction, but those in the group all knew, of course, who was meant. Marty and his wife, standing there.

"Every generation," Lynn thought, and shook his head.

The Minister's speech continued. Lynn heard a car on the road behind him.

He heard it slow down and stop, and one, then another door open. He looked back to see a man and woman in their seventies, farmers, or retired farmers from the look of them, dressed in their Sunday clothes, the man helping the woman, who was stepping carefully in her best shoes.

Lynn saw them walk to the fence of the cemetery, and debate silently whether to move the rail and chance disrupting the ceremony, and decide to stay, like Lynn, outside the fence. The man removed his hat. He and his wife listened to the Minister.

". . . has always said this: 'God is on our Side.' " The Minister said, "And it was not a statement of Faith, but a *boast;* for, how can we know . . ."

"The perfect cool day," Lynn thought. "And before the black flies. Isn't it lovely how we are reminded of the good by the bad? And who's to say . . ." He saw a stone house in Belgium. In the upper story window, which was just barely above his head, as he rode in the tank, the young woman with brown hair, and the large eyes, and the washed-out blue dress with the white collar, and she looked at him. "There was a life in that look," he thought, "and she knew it, and I knew it." And he thought of a girl in Chicago that one time. He glanced over at the old couple, as the Minister finished his speech, and rejoined the group.

Lynn caught Marty's eye, and tilted his head toward the old couple, and he and Marty pulled back the bar, and Marty motioned them forward into the group. They nodded their thanks and Marty inclined his head toward Lynn to say: "Thank you for bringing it to my attention."

The twelve-year-old girl came forward. She wore a white dress and a red windbreaker which, to judge by the wear, must necessarily be a hand-me-down.

"No, you don't see that color anywhere," he thought. "Once in a while, once in a while, on some tint of the maple leaf, that's right. That washed-out red. That's right."

"In Flanders Fields," the girl began.

"And probably b'longed to her brothers," Lynn thought. "Now, whose little girl is that?" He looked at her, at the wind puffing her white dress, and at the pond, down below the cemetery, and back at the girl, studying her features. "Well, I should be able to say, sure enough, for she sure looks like someone," he thought; "and if I *asked,* and they told me I would feel like a fool, for, I would say, 'Of *course,* she's, well, she's, looking like that, she's got to be . . .'" He pictured himself, thinking of the person he was picturing as an old man, who lived one or two generations in the past, and here was the child, who was the grandchild or it could be the great-grandchild of the kids he'd played with up the hill, and, yet, she could almost be them, looking like that. "*Dress* the same," he thought. "Dress in't no different. *Shoes*'re different. Jacket's different, she'd be wearin' some wool thing, some plaid, likely, but that would of belonged to her brothers, too, and maybe the shoes would, though they might have a time getting her into 'em, some high boots, if she was in her Sunday best.

". . . and what are Flanders Fields to us, today?" she said. "And what, to us, today, are the poppies that grew there?" She reached the end of a page, and put it at the bottom of her speech, and continued.

"She's doing *good*," Lynn thought. "Very good indeed. Sweet thing. Grow up, pretty quick, be someone's wife. Shame they didn't know the farm life."

". . . where the blood ran down and ran along the ground. In Springs like these," she said.

". . . Springs just like these," Lynn thought, "exactly like these. Idiots at the store talking about the weather. This and that. Of *course* it changes. Hell, I was a kid giving that speech, I'd say everything changes except War. That's what I'd say," he thought, and he was back in the old schoolhouse. "Damn fools to've torn it down," he thought, and the wooden desks with the iron scrollwork bolting them to the floor, and the glass inkwells, and the pink and green map of the World, and Mrs. Moultrie, "only one who liked me," he thought. "And did we come up here?" he thought. "Did we do that? Would we of done that . . . ?" The girl finished her speech and looked up, confused, for a brief moment, and was directed back into the group.

The Captain of the Color Guard gave a low command, and the two riflemen stepped forward. "Present *Arms*," he said, and the men did so. "Three rounds. On my command. Aim: *Fire*," and, then again, and then the third round which echoed back from across the pond. The two men executed an about-face, and rejoined the rank. The man on the left turned to the Captain, and showed Inspection Arms, the Captain took his carbine, and the man turned around. A woman in the crowd came forward and handed him the bugle. On command, the American Flag dipped slightly, and the man came forward and blew Taps. Two men in the crowd took their hats off. Lynn could smell the laundry detergent and the bleach in the little girl's dress.

"No, it's an art," he thought. "Moving men by command. What would it take to get them back to town? 'Bout Face, F'rrd march, Squad Right Wheel, n'that would do it."

"Always the unforeseen, though," he thought.

"Always the unforeseen."

The two of them sat in the deer camp, and the rain came down in a drizzle so fine you wouldn't have known it was raining if you didn't see it dripping off the tree.

They were dressed in wool. Old green wool trousers, and wool shirts washed to a softness like cashmere. The Trooper's shirt was tucked into his pants, deep red above the thick black belt. His friend's was grey and green, and draped over the back of his chair. He wore a torn, grey longsleeved cotton undershirt in a waffled weave, the sleeves pushed back over his thick forearms. He was hunched over the butt-end of a split maple log, upended underneath the window.

The revolver lay on the log. It was an old, blue Smith and Wesson .38 with checkered, walnut grips. The backsight was a simple channel milled into the topstrap; and the front, a half-round, just like half a nickel, soldered to the barrel.

The man pushed his glasses up on his forehead and leant closer to the gun, and sighed.

"N'l look in the jacket pocket, and there is the motel key," the Trooper said.

"Well," his friend said. "That's the way it is. Time goes by." He picked up the small rectangular box on the windowsill and read. " 'Clean area.' I did that. 'Apply generously with a . . .' " He nodded, to say, "What do you *want* of me . . . ?"

"What do you want with that antique, *anyway?*" the Trooper said.

"That's right," his friend said, absently, still reading. " 'Thoroughly cleanse all metal . . .' "

"You did that'm," the Trooper said.

" '. . . with fine-grit emery cloth, until . . .' "

The Trooper picked up the box. "It says, rinse it underneath the . . ."

"I know what it *says*, it just ain't *doin'* . . ."

"What the hell you want with that *antique*, for, anyway . . . ?"

"Well, yes, you said that," his friend said.

"You getting old?"

"Tha's what I want to tell you," his friend said. "You said, 'The motel key' . . . ? Well, look here, things change. You say she attacked you? Hell she *going* to do? People'll use the *weapons*, they think are appropriate." He picked the revolver up and looked at it. On the blade of the front sight, held parallel, flat, to the ground, a small bubble of liquid rested.

"Hell, it's rusting underneath the bubble," the man said.

The Trooper picked up the box and read. "Rinse it off," he said. His friend was up, and walked to the dry sink. He picked up the mason jar resting in it, and took it and the revolver out on the porch. He poured a bit of water over the blade of the sight, to rinse the bubble off. He held the gun up to examine it.

"I have fucked this into a fare-thee-well," he said.

He walked back in the cabin. The Trooper sat, still at the window, reading the instructions on the box. The older man took a kerchief from his back pocket and wiped down the sight, where rust was already beginning to form. "Fucked-up beyond recognition," he said.

The Trooper held the box. " 'The Liquid,' " he read, " 'and the firearm must be at Room Temperature, for the bluing compound to take effect' . . ." He looked up at the man, and they both stopped a moment.

"Many years as I've been doing this," his friend said. He took the maple log and carried it by the stove, and set it down, and the gun on top of it.

The Trooper took the small cylindrical bottle out of the box. "Y'wan'to heat this, too?"

"No, thing'll probably, we heat it, blow up, blow us all to hell, nobody know why," he said. "Well, *yeah*." He reached out his hand, and the Trooper put the bottle into it, and the man set it next to the revolver, on the maple log by the stove. He moved the log back a half-foot, and the two men sat there, backs to the open door, warmed by the fire, looking at the log with the gun and the bottle on it.

"*Cold* weather, you want to stay out of the Notch, up there," the older man said. "It heats *up*, n'*flood-ing* . . ."

The Trooper nodded. ". . . that's right," he said.

". . . where you want to be *then*," his friend finished,
". . . down on the *flats*."

The two men sat there, and each lit another cigarette. The Trooper tossed his match toward the stove. The older man rubbed his between his fingers, and dropped it on the floor. He looked at the soot on his fingers, and he wiped them on his woolen pants. He reached behind him, and shrugged himself into his shirt. They looked at the stove, the deep orange seen through the grate at the bottom.

"Well, hell, yes," the man said. "Any weapon to hand. *Anyone*. You think you wuu'n't . . . ?" The Trooper looked at him. "They ain't no *sportmanship*," the older man said. "No more'n a barroom fight. It ain't a boxing match. What people want, 'to Win.'

"Most people, you see . . . n'this is the difference, them n'us, never confront that. Go their ways. Rather not know it." He shook his head. "But you put somebody in a corner, *wrong* them, something . . ." He opened his mouth, slightly, and his tongue protruded in his cheek. "That person's going to have revenge.

"Muck up a *woman*, she is going to muck *you* up. Where'd you find th'motel key?"

"Last year's, light Uniform."

"Isn't that funny?" the man said. ". . . things disappear? Things show up, twenty-five years later . . . ? Inn't that funny . . . ?

"Yeauuppp," the Trooper said.

"I'll *tell* you," his friend said. "Fishin' hooks, Charlie *Taggart* gave me, f'teen *years* ago."

"Where?"

"Pocket a, some old *vest*..." his friend said, and swept his hand toward the wall of the shack, toward a row of hooks in the wall, which bore old coats, and hats, and a pair of snowshoes.

"Old *vest*," he said. "Must to've had it on, ten, twenty times since he died. And would've bet a brick house there's nothing in there. I come up, light the stove, yes'dy, loo'n for a *match*..." He mimed patting his chest pockets, and gestured at the hooks again, and shrugged, to say, "And there you have it."

"Pocket, vest, n'l remember, shit, fifteen *years* ago, fishing, *ice* fishing, Loach Dam. N'we din' even *use* the hooks. Charlie, he's fumblin', hands all cold, he drops his *gloves*, something..." His face brightened. "We're trine t'get the *stove* on. N'he's fumblin', his *hands*'re cold, digs in his pockets for some goddamn, something the *stove*... it wasn't the stove, it was the *Coleman* lamp; n'he says he's got a new *mantle*, and dropping stuff, the floor the shack, hands me the *hooks*... Of *course*, she's goin' to fight you," he continued. "D'you *think* that she was going to do? Shit. Begging your *pardon*," he said. "She finds that *key*, she's *got* to fight." He sighed.

"All right. We're going to try again," he said. He picked the log up gingerly, balancing the gun and the bottle on its end, and moved them back to their spot underneath the window. He opened the bottle of bluing, and dipped the corner of his kerchief in it, and spread it on the blade of the sight, evenly, on both sides. "You see?" he said.

"What you want with that old gun, *anyway*?" the young man said.

"Shoot it," his friend said.

"... you *pay* for it?"

His friend shrugged. "Hunnerd, Hunnerd-twenty. Bought it, up, last year, the Gun Show. Things different, then. Cop's gun. Holster wear" — he pointed to the gun, his witness — "rubbed the sight clean, but I doubt, things been shot, more'n a box, box or two, f'ty years. N'it's going to *shoot* good, too." He pointed at the young man, to put him in his place. "Fixed sights, not all this bullshit . . . little to the left. My *windage* . . . so on." He smiled.

"N'there's nothing wrong, *nostalgia*," the Trooper said.

"Well, shit," the old man said, "you *mock* me, what are *you* doin' here, but 'membering that *girl* . . . ?"

He picked up the revolver with one finger hooked through the open frame. He carried it out on the porch, and bent and took the water jar up, and poured water again, over the blade of the sight. He walked inside, and set the gun back down on the log.

"Throw tha. f'unn motel key away," the old man said.

"N'this Fish and *Game* patch," the Trooper said.

". . . mmm?"

". . . the same pocket. Uniform."

". . . mmm . . ."

"Marty Breen give me. Come up to me. Last year. At his boy's funeral. He said he found it in the woods. And could it be a *clue*. To that girl's disappearance."

". . . come up to you the funeral . . . ?"

"He said that it was plaguing his mind. That it

meant something," the Trooper said. "Fish and Game patch." He paused a moment. "Minnesota . . ."

"Out-of-towner? Killed her?" the old man said.

"Sm'b'y killed her, dragged her off . . . I don't know . . ."

"Shit, that girl just *walked* off, I think," The old man said.

"I don't know. Maybe. Didn't *take* anything, f'she did."

"Maybe, just wanted, leave it behind . . ."

"Or wen' off, somewhere, someone, got in his car . . ." The Trooper nodded. "Here or there, what difference?"

"Well, that's one way, look at it," the Trooper said. " 'Nyway, *she* ain't coming back."

"No. Wouldn't say so," his friend said.

"Li'l white fish on a cotton patch. Gon' solve th'secrets of the age," the Trooper said, and shook his head.

"And we would sit there, in that old ice-fishing shack," the old man said. "And he would tell me stories. Early days, the Village, the Town, Forest Service. And drink," he said, "And sit there. Room all fulla the *kerosene* . . ." The Trooper nodded, appreciative, in rhythm to his friend's litany; and the old man, buoyed by the accompaniment, prolonged it. ". . . the *smoke*, the *ice* smell, *you* know; cheap fucken *cigar* . . . stories, the War, the *Woods* . . . He found a man one time, he said, the woods; rifle right by him, leanin' 'gainst the tree, life crushed out of him."

"And what was that?" the young man said.

"He *said*," his friend said, "puzzled him no end. His

theory, black bear, come up, behind him . . ." The man portrayed a bear, reaching from behind a tree, to crush the man. "And killed him," he said. "But you *know,* I didn't think he should of told that story. How did he know it was a bear? Or, I'll tell you *what:* I'm not sure that it was true. It ought not to've been true, or, if it was true, he shouldn't of told it that way."